THE CURIOUS CASE OF FLORENCE WINTERS

MAY BRIDGES

The Curious Case of Florence Winters
© May Bridges 2021.
First Edition.
All rights reserved. No part of this story may be used, reproduced or transmitted in any form or by any means without written permission of the copyright holder, except in the case of brief quotations embodied within critical reviews and articles.
This book is a work of fiction. The names, characters, places, and incidents are products of the writer's imagination or have been used fictitiously and are not to be construed as real. Any resemblance to persons, living or dead, actual events, locale or organizations is entirely coincidental.
The author has asserted his/her rights under the Copyright Designs and Patents Acts 1988 (as amended) to be identified as the author of this book.
Cover design by Cozy Cover Designs - Molly Burton

Join May's newsletter and receive the prequel story, A Letter Most Curious, absolutely free!

THE CURIOUS CASE OF FLORENCE WINTERS

A KIDNAPPING in New York City's illustrious high society, and the inquisitive young woman who's determined to redeem her family's good name. Will she outsmart the culprit, even after another person winds up dead?

New York City, 1925.

Florence Winters is ready to escape the whispers about her.

Stuck in small-town Ohio, she's done living the spinster life and ready to move on to greener pastures, so when her wealthy and slightly eccentric Aunt Julia requests Florence's companionship in New York City—she knows it's an offer she can't refuse.

But she has no idea what awaits her in Aunt Julia's ravishing brownstone in the West Village. Secret meetings. Secret passages. Secretive house staff. Even Aunt Julia's cat seems to have something to hide!

Florence isn't the type to pry, but when one of Aunt Julia's affluent adversaries ends up missing and another is found dead, Aunt Julia is suspected of foul play. Florence feels she owes it to her hostess to search for the truth... even if it means putting herself in the dangerous crosshairs of a murderer.

The Curious Case of Florence Winters is the first in the Florence Winters Mystery series - a historical cozy mystery series set in the 1920s. *They're full of alluring twists and lovely characters. If you'd like to know more about what Downton Abbey's own Lady Grantham's life was like back in America, this is the series for you.*

1

October 13, 1925

The train shuddered to a tumultuous stop with a hiss. Florence Winters opened her eyes, startled by the cold chill pressed against them. Even through the fogginess, she realized that she'd fallen asleep somewhere between Cleveland and Pittsburgh, slumbering away while any manner of things could've transpired without her knowledge. How long had that been? Had they finally arrived at her destination?

The train's shrill whistle shot through her bleariness, through her confusion, through her very nerves.

She started, her black felt cloche tilted slightly askew as she pulled away from the cold pane of glass. Long brown tendrils of hair had escaped their pinnings, now damp from the glass reflecting her mussed look.

Oh, for heaven's sake! She couldn't arrive to such a thing, looking as though she'd only just woken up. It would surely get back to her mother, and Martha Winters was always around the corner with a proper tongue-lashing.

Quick to tuck her hair back up the best she could, Florence slipped on her warm leather gloves and stood up, adjusting her hat until it fit just right. She glanced toward the fogged glass again, training her eyes on the people crossing the platform. All of them had different lives being pulled in different directions. Could any of them be as nervous as she was? Her heartbeat was a flurry as it twitched inside her chest.

She placed a gloved hand against the wet glass, satisfied at the print it left behind. It would be the only way to leave her mark on this part of her journey, other than the ticket stub she remembered to stash away in her coat pocket.

The train's wide window was the only thing separating her from her new life, a thought that went from a whisper to a screeching reality. Florence imagined her future as she clutched her purse, silently begging for it be true.

Past the steady traffic of people beyond the window, she tried to make out the sign hanging along the brick archway of the platform. *Grand Central, Platform 12.*

She'd made it after all.

Quickly scooping up the belongings she'd brought inside the car with her, she followed the handful of others waiting to depart. There was a nervous energy in the train car, but perhaps it was just hers.

There was no way of knowing what to expect when she stepped off the train, but boy, nothing could've prepared her for how *loud* it was.

Porters yelling up and down the platform outside the many train cars. Half a dozen newsboys rushing along the crowd, shoving the evening newspaper into hands. A woman chasing a gaggle of shrieking children deeper into the crowd. White steam wheezing above them all, billowing out from the trains on each track.

Florence wasn't sure whether she wanted to plug her ears or stand back and watch the busy people of New York City.

"Hey lady, why don't you watch it? We're walking here!" a man in a fur cap with a cigarette dangling from his mouth yelled at Florence in a rough accent, handling one end of a steamer trunk twice the size of hers behind him while another man handled the other end. They both shook their heads at her and retreated deeper into the crowd.

She ducked out of the way of others, trying to peer over heads to find where her luggage went. Judging by the line, she'd find it past the reluctant mass of people.

She recognized the porter from the train and watched as he was quick to check off each person ahead of her, giving each luggage tag a hasty onceover. "Next!"

Florence blinked, realizing that meant her. "Oh!" She rushed up to him, clutching her heavy scarlet wool coat around her. "Sorry, sir."

"Name?"

"Florence Winters. Those would be mine right there, sir, the brown steamer trunk and the smaller brown suitcases," she said, pointing beside him.

He looked her up and down, took her ticket, and fumbled for the luggage tags. "Winters. Here ya go."

Florence stumbled forward as he pushed everything toward her, but she thanked him through gritted teeth anyway and dragged all of her belongings through the crowd of people milling around the platform. Where were the trolleys? Surely someone had a way of carrying their things that didn't involve tripping over their own two feet!

Despite the mid-October chill, Florence found a place to sit, practically perspiring. The whistling of another train pulling into the station hissed through the air. She jolted.

The city of dreams... at least that was what her friend Bernice had called it when Florence had told her the news. *'What a steal! Imagine leaving dumpy old Jebediah-Ahiya for the big city!'* Bernice had squealed, her eyes not giving away an edge of jealousy. *'This is it, this is what you've been waiting for, Flo!'*

Her friend's excitement didn't surprise her at all. It was easy enough for Bernice to get excited about things, and just as easy enough for Florence to be cautious. It was true that she was dying to leave that dusty old town behind, and it was true there was no better place to try to get your writing published than in New York City. But in her dreams, she'd always thought her hopeful getaway would be on her own terms, and not those set for her by others. No matter how generous those terms were.

It wasn't that she was opposed to getting out of Jebediah. In those dreams, she was living on her own near Akron, a stone's throw from where she worked as a telephone operator. Those dreams pulled her through the hot and busy days in the telephone exchange, where her throat grew raspy by the end of her shift. On her short breaks, she'd close her eyes and imagine this new life she'd eagerly lead.

There was always a bungalow, a home to be spoken for. And sometimes, there was even a handsome young gentleman in his Sunday best, leaning over the porch rail to steal a quick kiss from his bride.

But without a wedding band on her finger there was no way to find a place to rent on her own, much less a bungalow buy.

Instead she was stuck living with her family, an arrangement that left both her and her mother unhappy.

The same woman from before passed by and grabbed hold of her oldest child's arm, yanking him back toward her, her face grim as the other handful of children stopped short. "You'll mind me or so help me, you'll go to bed hungrier than the street rats tonight!"

That seemed to do the trick. The rest of them fell in line and marched after their mother with sour looks on their pink faces.

Mothers could be fickle even at the best of times, Florence decided. Martha Winters had four children but seemed to only focus her attentions on one of them—Florence.

While her older sister, Anna, was able to do and say as she pleased with their mother, Florence had to mind her steps quite literally.

'Anna is only three years older, Florence, yet look at how well she's done for herself. Married to a doctor and blessing me with that beautiful little Amos! Maybe if you put yourself out there more. Pastor Finchley has a nephew who just moved closer to the church...'

'What about the boys?' Florence would usually pipe up. Her younger twin brothers had only recently graduated from

school and were the rotten apples of her mercurial mother's eye.

'They're working with your father, naturally. You know he's teaching them to take over Winters Fine Tailoring one day. And they're young men with their lives ahead of them. What do they have to do with anything?'

Florence always made it a point to bite her tongue when it came to her mother. There was no use in attempting to twist her way out of an argument with that woman. Martha had made it clear that Florence was well on her way to spinsterhood at the ripe old age of twenty-three.

Which made the sudden change in her life all the more perplexing.

Here she was, saving up what little she could to one day exchange this dull life for something more exciting, when she found a letter that had been stashed away in her mother's writing desk, addressed to Florence herself. A letter that Mother had failed to hand over.

In elegant script had been her Aunt Julia's request for Florence to move into her lavish brownstone row house in New York City's affluent Greenwich neighborhood as a companion and head of household. She couldn't imagine anything further from her current life or anything more beguiling.

A wealthy aunt inviting her niece to live in what she considered an American castle was like something out of one of Florence's favorite novels. Why her? And why did Aunt Julia need a companion? Uncle Albert had died five years ago, and she hadn't remarried—and who would? When you're one of the richest women in the country, there was hardly a need for a husband.

And why in the world had Mother opened the letter in the first place? The circumstances were murky at best, and no one in the family was willing to give Florence much to go on. So she was to be sent to the big city without anyone taking her feelings on the matter into consideration... and that was that.

All of it led up to her sitting on the bench under a large standing clock, trying to remember if she was to meet someone outside the massive terminal hall. Something told her she may have missed her aim.

"Miss Winters?" A voice called out, almost unheard in the din of the space. A young man in a heavy tweed coat and chauffeur cap gave her a little wave to catch her attention.

Apprehension bloomed across her chest as Florence stood up. "Yes?"

He nodded, tipping his cap at her, and pushed a trolley between them. "I'm Benjamin—Benny, that is. I'll be taking you back to Mrs. Bryant's home."

She chewed the inside of her cheek, a bad habit that left the skin sore and raw even after she ran her tongue along it. It occurred to her that maybe she should ask a few more questions before trusting this Benny fellow. "And how are you so sure that I'm who you're looking for?"

"You're the only one sitting still," he said, flashing Florence a hooked smile. She caught sight of an endearing chipped tooth. "Everyone else is moving and rushing, but you're sitting and waiting. No one sits and thinks around here, you know. It's Florence, right?"

Despite the roar of people around them, Benny's accent was really something—a little rough around the edges—but warm and friendly all the same. Her name carried a certain cadence coming from him, and it almost tempted her into asking him to repeat it. She bit back the urge to do so and nodded instead, his smile growing even wider as she did.

"Then it's settled. I know you, you know me. We're not strangers anymore and I'll get you out of here and into somewhere a little less crowded."

"Is my aunt waiting for me? I... I wasn't sure whether she'd be meeting me here or not." She fidgeted with the smaller suitcase's handle.

"Mrs. Bryant coming to meet you here?" He squinted his dark eyes at her, the corner of his mouth quirking up again as if he expected her to be teasing him. With a chuckle, Benny took his cue. "Sorry, Miss Winters, but coming to pick you up is *my* job, and yes, she's back home waiting for you. I expect she's pretty swell on seeing you right about now."

If she were being honest with herself—and Florence considered herself to be an honest person—she hadn't the slightest fancy of how Aunt Julia might have felt about her. She could scarcely remember the last time she'd even seen her. The older woman tended to keep to herself.

"All right." She released her tight grip on the smaller suitcase and lugged it on top of the larger one that Benny had just placed on the trolley.

He pulled the trolley toward him with a shake of his head. She could just make out the dark wavy hair peeking out from underneath the chauffeur cap.

"I've got this, no worries. It's all part of the job, yeah?" he said. "Just follow me."

He made a rather convincing argument. She watched as he finished loading up the trolley with her things, until he gestured for her to keep up.

"Your aunt's expecting us so we should probably get moving."

She glanced around the large building, taking in the heavy columns, the heavy windows, and the heavy heat hanging right above their heads despite the chilliness outside. There were just so many people. Florence had never seen such a crowd rushing about like this, even in downtown Akron, even in the telephone operation department, even during the county bazaars.

Folks were milling past them on both sides, paying her no mind other than the twinge of annoyance on some of their faces in passing, probably from her being smack dab in the middle of their journeys.

She dashed after Benny, purse clutched at her side.

When they finally made it outside past the throng of people, the chill of mid-October pushed against her like the tide. But she was far too occupied to worry herself over it.

Now, Florence thought she might've had a proper understanding of the word *overwhelming*. She did grow up with a bossy older sister and twin terrors for little brothers, after all. That was before she stepped outside, however, her heels hardly audible clicking against the New York City pavement.

The cacophony of the city surrounded her on every side, with a wreath of sound flooding her every thought, invading her every sense, and washing over her every word until they drowned in her throat, unsaid.

She wasn't sure she could process so much at once. Luckily, she didn't have to. Right out in front of them was a stunning automobile Benny was hightailing it to, careful not to hit the trolley against it as he sidled up to unload the luggage.

The long sky-blue body was trimmed in gold and polished until it shone. There were plenty of Tin Lizzies back home, but she'd never seen such a brightly colored automobile in her life.

She quirked an eyebrow at it. "This is your car?"

Benny let out a deep chuckle, unloading her suitcases. "I wish. No, this is Mrs. Bryant's latest. She's a fan of the blue. Thinks it's a beauty."

"I don't think I've ever thought of a car as being beautiful, but I guess I've been proven wrong," she said. "Aunt Julia has good taste."

"Don't I know it. If you think the machine's something, wait until you get a look at the house. Full trimming everywhere you look. It's a showstopper, easy." The roar from a line of cars drowned out the other half of what Benny said, but Florence was too busy to notice.

The sky above was crowded in a way she'd never seen before; tall buildings seemed to tower over them. The deep blue of early twilight was just spreading and with it several cars' headlights flickered to life.

She tilted her head back, taking in the building from which they had just come out of. *Grand Central Terminal* was etched into the cream-colored stone underneath a beautifully sculpted scene.

"That statue up there," she said, pointing to a man in a winged helmet and his companions chiseled in the light stone. "Do you know what it's of? It's hard to get a good look at it from down here."

Benny scratched at his cap. "Mercury, if memory serves. It was all over the newspapers when they finished building this place. I was just a kid. That's Hercules and Minerva, too. Don't know much else about them other than that," he said, opening the rear passenger door for her.

"They're Roman gods. Well, Minerva was a goddess, of course, and Hercules was a demi-god. Half-god, half-human, that is. Mercury was the Roman god of wealth and trade, Minerva, the goddess of wisdom, poetry, and music, among other things. Hercules was a human in some versions, half-god in others. He had to complete the twelve labors, which were sort of like trials he faced against monsters and..." she trailed off, blood rushing to burn at her cheeks. If she had a penny for every time she'd gone off on a literary tangent...

But Benny didn't seem to be put off by any of it. In fact, his good-natured grin had returned. "If I could be talented at even one of those things, I'd be doing all right. You seem to know a lot about that kind of thing."

"I'm certainly no expert on Roman mythology, but I've always found the stories fascinating. I'm a bit of a book-reader, you see." It was silly to find this embarrassing, but it had always seemed to put whoever she was talking with to sleep. Particularly if the other person was Bernice.

"A smart gal, then." Benny closed the door and she settled into her seat, somewhat awestruck at both the scenery and Aunt Julia's chauffeur. She only hoped everyone else she met along this odd new journey of hers would be as amiable.

"It won't be long. We're only a few miles away," Benny called from the front as the car rumbled to life beneath their feet. "Just down 7th and Leroy."

Florence had no idea where any of that was, but she stared up at the sky anyway, imagining.

People streamed up and down the sidewalks, avoiding the many cars crowding the street. There was store after store, and the smell of motor oil and yeasty dough filled the air as they passed a delicatessen. A large library on the corner gave way to a sprawling cemetery and in front of it, a line of brick and brown row houses lined the street. It was in front of Number Seven where Benny eased the car into an empty space.

As soon as she was free from the car, she clapped her hand to her hat to avoid losing it in a gust of chilly wind. Dry leaves skittered past her feet toward the steps and she was looking hard and thinking harder, trying to piece this together.

Her father's older sister in need of companionship, was what started it. But now Florence couldn't help but wonder what life was like on the other side of the front door.

2

The door opened before she had the chance to reach toward the knob and behind it an older man with a perfectly pressed butler's uniform and out-of-fashion white beard stood to the side, bowing. "Miss Winters." He had the look of someone who held himself in high esteem, with little regard for anyone else.

Florence smiled and stuck out her hand, anyway. "Pleased to meet you."

He eyed her hand as if it were coiled up and ready to strike him. "I'm Hamish, Mrs. Bryant's butler. She's waiting to meet with you in the reception room." His thick Scottish accent caught on the *r's* in a disarming way and she slowly dropped her hand. Even though Florence was easily the same height, he sure did shrink her down for size.

As the steamer trunk bumped against the steps behind her, she noticed his eye twitch ever so slightly. "Benjamin, you know where to put those." When he turned to her, his expression smoothed over. "And you may follow me."

Sneaking a glance past him, she chewed at her bottom lip, a habit that she couldn't seem to break. "I'm ready when you are." It just so happened to be the first lie she'd told in a while. Unless you counted the fib about Mother's choice in perfumes. No one should go around smelling like dead flowers at a funeral.

Hamish let her past and she clutched even tighter to her favorite scarlet coat, a thread of jittery nerves threatening to undo the rest of her.

Words escaped her as soon as she really looked around inside.

The whole room seemed to bloom in front of her at once. Intricate polished wood was cherry dark and shining against the massive crystal chandelier hanging above their heads. There were fresh flowers on many surfaces; the scent of gardenias tickled her nose as she took a few more timid steps.

An ornately carved clock stood guard next to the grand staircase ahead. She gasped as her gaze swept up the staircase furnished in a velvety red to match the wood. At the first landing, stained glass in every shade imaginable winked at her in the dying sunlight.

Barely more than a dozen feet into the house, and Florence was in love. It felt like more than some wealthy person's home—though she wouldn't rule that out yet—but rather a museum of high society.

It had the look of an elegant manor house set somewhere in the English countryside, and she sighed at the thought. Was there a tea room? If there was a tea room, and she very much hoped there was, she wondered what kind of tea she'd pick. Mother wasn't much of a tea drinker, so

Florence really had no sense of what flavor she might like to try…

Hamish cleared his throat. "If you would, Miss Winters."

The wide mirror beside them reflected her startled look, and she snapped her gaping mouth shut. She didn't want Hamish to think her some kind of country bumpkin, much less Aunt Julia. "Of course, I apologize. It's just such a lovely home."

He puffed out his chest a little more, pride etched on his face. "I'm sure Mrs. Bryant would love to hear your appreciation."

The vestibule they stood in branched out to the left and right as well as opening to the grand hall, and she noticed a set of small stairs going down the right side, mainly because a very fat orange cat sat on the top step eyeing her with lazy interest.

A cat! Papa was allergic to them so they were never allowed to have any in the house, though plenty roamed the streets mewling at all hours of the night. She smiled at it, giving it a little wave before following Hamish.

But she was startled when she stopped short to look at a gorgeous gazing glass and was promptly bumped into from behind.

"I'm so sorry, Miss Winters. I promise I'm not a complete klutz," Benny groaned as he went to move the suitcase out of his way. "Are you all right?"

She waved a gloved hand at him. "Don't be silly. I'm fine."

Hamish had already walked ahead into what must have been the reception room, but she smiled at Benny, darting her eyes toward the stairs. "I would ask you if you needed help but something tells me I might incur someone's wrath if I do," she said with a smirk.

"Good instincts." He shook his head and smiled before turning back to make his way up the staircase.

There was another impatient noise coming from the room and Florence drew in a deep breath, fumbled with the black celluloid buttons down the front of her coat—now too warm for her to wear inside—and walked in after him.

It was childish to be so on edge about something as simple as meeting with her aunt, but it couldn't be helped. Julia Bryant held more power in her little finger than any man in town thanks to her late husband founding the largest timber, lumber, and paper company in the country—it both terrified and amazed Florence.

It was a hard thing to keep her chin up as she spotted the woman sitting in a high-backed chair, but somehow she pulled it off as she strolled in with a hopeful smile. "Good evening, Aunt Julia."

The older woman rose, her cool gaze settled into a polite expression. "Florence, it's so lovely to see you again. I trust your trip was uneventful?"

Florence nodded. "It was a dream." She failed to mention the part where she slept most of the way.

"I'm glad to hear it. Come closer, dear. You mustn't skulk about in doorways."

The words reeled her in like a fishing line and the next thing she knew she was closely under her aunt's observant gaze. Aunt Julia may have been sizing her up, but Florence was making mental notes, too.

Being tall must've run in the family with Aunt Julia easily an inch or two taller. Her dark blue eyes were cut through with warm brown, the same color as Papa's, and she wore his same prominent chin. And yes, Florence couldn't help but notice her aunt was, as Bernice's voice seemed to snicker in her ear, *'blessed in the bosom,'* which must *not* have run in the family.

Her silvery hair was elegantly rolled up away from her striking face in a style that suggested she was timeless, a theme Florence was noticing inside Number Seven, St. Luke's Place. From the Irish lace collar and navy silk afternoon gown to the buttoned boots peeking out from under her skirts, her aunt was perfectly in fashion with the rest of the place.

There was something about her that Florence thought was almost dominating, though she couldn't quite figure out why. Maybe the way she held her posture or the way she seemed to tower over her, even though Florence herself was hardly petite. It was apparent Aunt Julia's words carried weight with everyone no matter who she was speaking to, but more importantly, so did her silence.

Florence worked to keep the smile on her face from wilting. "It's been a long time since we've seen each other."

"Too long, I'm afraid," Aunt Julia agreed. "My affairs keep me rather busy so I'm not afforded much leisure time. Your father hopefully understands."

She quickly nodded. "Of course! Papa is busy all the time with the shop, so I'm sure he does. This home of yours," Florence glanced around, taking in the warm and lavishly decorated room, "I'm not at all surprised it keeps you busy."

Aunt Julia did something unexpected and smiled. "It is not typically the house I am dealing with, as that's left to Hamish and Virginia. I have other things that require my attention since I'm on different community boards and the like. You'll find out soon enough that a woman in a position like mine doesn't cease to exist when her husband passes on."

"I would never assume such a thing," Florence said quietly.

Aunt Julia gave a stiff nod, but took her hand and gently squeezed. "I would hope not. Now I'm sure you've had a long journey and would like to rest. Hamish can show you to your quarters. I hope they are to your taste. Chef serves dinner at six o'clock but given the circumstances, I believe seven thirty would work best this evening."

"Oh. All right, then. I'll see you at dinner." Florence could only smile. A chef! Of course there would be a chef. She couldn't really picture Aunt Julia looking over boiling pots with not a hair out of place. Naturally, her stomach rumbled at the mention of food and she blushed, hoping she was the only one who noticed.

She followed Hamish out without another word, a little dazed from it all. Her quarters, it turned out, were at the very top of the wide spiraling flights of stairs, on the fourth floor.

Hamish pulled open the double doors, and it was like walking into a new world. While the sitting room of the home was timeless, elegant, and dark, the massive bedroom was something completely different.

The room was straight out of the latest *Harper's Bazaar* edition and, in fact, Florence was certain she'd seen some of the contents of her new room inside one of the magazines.

Instead of dark wood, the room was airy and light, even colorful. She half expected a model in some fancy Chanel evening frock to come strolling through, decked to the nines and ready for a night out.

"You can ring for one of us there," Hamish spoke up, pointing to a buzzer next to the light switch on the wall. "If you need anything, that is. Dinner will be ready at seven thirty, as Mrs. Bryant promised. Will you need a reminder call?"

She blinked. "A reminder call?"

"To let you know when to come down?"

This seemed a funny thing to ask, but she kept a straight face. "No, thank you. I'll make sure to watch the time."

He nodded and left her to it, quietly shutting the door.

The sitting room was partitioned off from the rest of the room by a wood-and-glass inlaid screen with the same curved arches and fanned scallops that were splashed across everything else. And she even had her own radio in the sitting room!

Past it was a room that truly deserved the French name 'boudoir.' A silver bed frame with the biggest bed she'd ever laid eyes on was front and center in the room, everything else set to match and complement it. Chic bed linens matched the curtains in creams and peaches. A beautiful green jade clock sat on top of a long and narrow writing desk with a matching chair. Above the very middle of the room was a chandelier that hung in scalloped swaths of elegant crystal.

There was a door here and, oh—she had her own lavatory in her own room! It, too, had a very chic look to it with its green jade and creamy porcelain fixtures. A large tub would fit Florence completely when she went to draw a bath. The light floral-scented potpourri made her want to take a long, hot bath right now, but there wasn't enough time, and she refused to be late. That would never do.

It took her a moment to realize that there was yet another door in her room, and when she opened it she gasped, peeking her head inside for just a moment.

Oh no, she would have to devote much more time to what was inside the closet *after* dinner. Her clothes would be perfectly fine for her first evening here, after all. And Florence didn't need all of this to go to her head at once. Though the thought was tempting...

The windows let in the last of the light from the day, and she felt a sort of strange relief come over her. She was here, and this was all truly happening. It was no longer just some faraway dream.

She made a beeline to the gorgeous silver bed where her luggage was waiting for her. It was all she could do to keep from giggling as she flopped backward, unladylike.

Florence could see Bernice's face now, fawning over every last detail with her. "No doubt she'd have kittens over this," she murmured to herself with a laugh.

She brought the back of her fist up to her mouth, her eyes wide. How was this her life now? One minute she was stuck inside a loud room all day with her fellow operators, listening through the crackling air as she put people on the line through to their intended, and then the next minute she was holed up in a room that belonged in the Ritz-Carlton with dinner being prepped by a professional chef several floors below her.

Some might guess it was luck, but Florence knew there was more to the story than anyone was letting on. She was hopeful she'd get the chance to speak with Aunt Julia about the nature of her letter tonight.

At home it had been quite the mystery, with Florence and her mother practically at each other's throats when she found out the letter requesting her companionship—whatever that meant—was being kept from her.

She blew out a sigh. Secrets. She was never very fond of them, and she always seemed to find the truth somewhere along the line, hurtful or not. Florence had a knack for knowing when someone was lying to her. Bernice always called it her sixth sense, and would sulk any time Florence caught her trying to fib.

"Let's hope that Aunt Julia's as straightforward as she seems."

3

It took some doing, but Florence managed to pull herself from the comfort of a new mattress and silky sheets and dress for dinner. The steamer trunk popped open under her fingers, showcasing her most valuable belongings that she couldn't bear to part with.

It wasn't much. Just a few framed photos of her family and her dear Bernice, a bottle of Shalimar, and her favorite books... including her own notebooks full of writing that would never be read by anyone. Her desire to become the next great American novelist was a deep one, though usually she argued with herself over whether it was even a possibility. There were book publishers with headquarters in the city—a thought not lost on her. Aunt Julia *did* wield power and persuasion, though Florence had no idea how far of a reach she might possess. It seemed silly to even contemplate such things.

She took a deep breath, the scent of the lemon-and-bergamot perfume wafting over her, and pulled everything out to lay across the bed.

To her, there was nothing wrong with only holding on to what you cherished most and leaving the rest. Besides, she was perfectly happy to escape from the dreary clutches of sleepy Jebediah, Ohio. And the more she thought about it, the more pleased she became... it was hard not to with this step up in the world!

"What do you wear to a fancy dinner?" she wondered aloud as she pulled back a few choices. It wasn't a dinner party by any means, so it wouldn't be too formal.

There was the deep green cotton dress with gold embroidery around the collar and dropped hemlines and pleated skirt. It was a favorite of hers and one she and Mother had actually worked on together. Florence wasn't quite as skilled with the Singer as her mother, but she was a darn sight better than her sister Anna, who had one time managed to sew her sleeve to a curtain panel.

Though at closer inspection, the green did look rather faded. She tossed it to the side and picked up the soft cotton plaid dress with the wide matching belt, tilting it toward the light. It was frayed around the edges, though oddly enough she had never noticed until now.

"That's because it's hardly mattered until now, old girl," she noted to herself. "And, well, you can't go downstairs looking like a ragamuffin in front of everyone." It occurred to her just then that she had no idea who all 'everyone' entailed. There was Hamish and Aunt Julia, Benny, and someone named Virginia. Was that it, or should she expect more guests? At any rate, she figured it didn't matter; she was dressing to impress her aunt, of course. After all, she was here because of her graciousness.

"It looks like it's time to bring in the showstopper. How else could I possibly compare?"

The showstopper was the best dress she had—a hand-embroidered velveteen frock in midnight blue. She'd only worn it on two occasions: once to Bernice's engagement party, and once to the job interview at American Telephone and Telegraph for the switchboard operator position she'd held for the last three years. It was still in prime condition, and she did love the way the color complemented her paler complexion.

Slipping out of her traveling clothes and into the dress, she blew a strand of hair from her face—she'd have to redo it, too.

She went in front of the standing mirror in the corner of the room and admired the cut of the dress, turning this way and that, twisting her mouth to one side. "This will have to do." It didn't help that she was itching to get her hands on what was inside the closet.

At exactly five minutes until dinnertime, she began to make her way down the many steps, wishing she had time to tour the house. The gorgeous stained glass was enough to distract her, and she was glad to finally make it to the main floor without a moment to spare.

A woman with a head full of fiery ringlets pinned underneath a white headband met her at the bottom of the steps. Her plain black dress with starched white collar and matching apron led Florence to believe that this was Virginia.

The woman gave a curtsy with a small smile on her petite face. "Miss Winters. I'm Virginia, Mrs. Bryant's housemaid. Follow me to the dining room, if you would, Miss."

Florence nodded. "It's nice to meet you, Virginia. And thank you—I haven't had the chance to take a look around, so naturally I have no idea where to go."

The housemaid's smile drew wide. "It's no trouble. I'm sure you'll get the hang of it after a while. A word of caution though," Virginia began as she stopped short. "Auguste is trying to impress tonight, and he's a firm believer in the marriage of seafood and baked goods."

Florence blinked. "Auguste? Is he... the chef? And what do you mean *the marriage of seafood and baked goods*?"

Virginia bit her lip. "My apologies, Miss. Auguste is our chef, yes. And I only mean to say that the kitchen was smelling rather..." she trailed off with a wince, "undesirable. Sometimes he gets a recipe in his mind that he refuses to let go of until everyone has properly suffered its consequences —sorry—has delighted in its *new and interesting flavors*."

Florence let out a soft snort, unable to help herself. "Why do I have a feeling those are the chef's own words?"

The cheeky grin Virginia sported slipped into something more somber as they walked past a pair of wide double doors. "Mr. Bryant's study."

"Oh? Does Aunt Julia still use it?" She drew up in her mind the sort of room a wealthy businessman like her deceased uncle would conduct his affairs in. Papa's own office was a tiny room in the back of the tailor shop that had a propensity for mice through the winter.

Virginia shook her head. "It's the same as it was on the last day he sat in his chair. Though I keep it in order," she said, dropping her voice with another curtsy as they approached the dining room.

It was larger than all three of the bedrooms and the lavatory at home, put together. The ceiling felt sky-high and three wide-set chandeliers hung over the longest table Florence had ever seen. The massive windows looked out toward the street on one wall, and the corner of the block on the other wall, and Hamish was busy drawing the heavy draperies closed against the night.

Paintings of fruit spanned the room, and off to the side there was a tall portrait on display of Uncle Albert standing behind a younger Aunt Julia. In the portrait, she was seated in a chair overlooking the rest of the room, her eyes a steady gaze giving the appearance that she oversaw the dining table an all seated there. A long wedding veil trailed behind her, sweeping down and around by the white silk dress pooled at her feet. The sleeves billowed out before tapering tightly at the elbows, and the high collar bore a gorgeous cameo brooch. All of it put together revealed a stunning young woman who, quite frankly, was in a world all her own compared to the stoic Uncle Albert, whom Florence knew to be several years older.

Heavy, expensive candlesticks with their wicks flickering in flame and more fresh flowers adorned the long table. The soft, sweet scent of hydrangeas complemented the nearly black dahlias. Strange. Florence was sure they were already out of season. Did Aunt Julia have access to her own greenhouse for whatever flowers she'd like? Somehow, that didn't seem out of the realm of possibility.

At least the *undesirable* smell Virginia had referred to had yet to make its debut.

Aunt Julia sat at one end of the table and smiled the same polite smile as earlier, gesturing for Florence to take a seat. "You look lovely, dear. That color is quite fetching. The chef has prepared us a special dinner from what I've been told, though I'm afraid I will have to retire early afterward."

Hamish seemed to materialize out of nowhere at Florence's side to pull out her seat. She thanked him and looked at the giant wooden clock hanging over the fireplace's mantel with a frown. "Are you feeling unwell?"

She wasn't sure how early Aunt Julia went to bed, but Florence herself was every bit awake as she could be until at least ten thirty. It was something that had always bunched up Mother's skirts.

Aunt Julia, however, wasn't affected by her question. "No, I am fine. I have a few things to tend to this evening, is all. You won't be needing my company tonight, will you?"

When she phrased it that way, Florence felt a little silly for even asking. "Not at all, Auntie." And then she felt even more like a kid when Aunt Julia lifted an eyebrow in her direction. "Sorry. Not at all, Aunt Julia," she corrected. "Though... I did want to speak to you about something, if you don't mind."

The elder woman carefully tucked her napkin across her lap. "Of course, dear."

"It's about your letter. You see, it was never really explained to me what my purpose is here. Mother wasn't..." she trailed off, not wanting to seem like a petulant child tattling on someone, "*sure* if you meant for me to work in the house or what being your companion entailed. And I'd hoped to know sooner rather than later so that I might prepare myself. I don't mind putting in hard work." It was the simple truth, although a tiny voice inside her loudly hoped that wasn't the case.

"I see. You've had a good look around your quarters I'm willing to bet."

Florence nodded.

"Then I'm sure you've put together that you're here as my guest and not as my servant. I have a good eye for judging a person, Florence. You are very observant. I gather not much gets past you. Though I appreciate your willing work ethic, it will not be required." She smiled again, taking a careful sip from her glass.

Well, at least there was that. "And being your companion? Is that... does that mean anything specific?"

At this, her aunt took time to answer. "Think of it as your pass to domestic freedom. I see myself as your way forward, however you wish that way to be. You're a woman with gumption who's smart and able-bodied. I have need for more ladies in my company like that. Though your companionship is more for your sake than mine, I must admit."

She mulled the words over, scrounging up the right thing to say. But all Florence could think was how wonderfully generous this subtle yet freeing offer had truly been. It had slipped under the radar of Mother, who'd seen Florence's stay in New York as a way in for marriage, and she knew Papa would be fine with whatever she wanted either way.

"I take those words as a high compliment coming from such an intelligent person," she said, giving her aunt the most appreciative smile she could muster.

"Ah, Auguste!" Aunt Julia said in delight as she bit into her roasted *chateaubriand*. "He's such a masterful chef. Have you tried your dish yet?"

"I haven't, though I think I'll remedy that now."

Dinner was a rather quiet affair after that, with Aunt Julia looking up now and then to ask her how she was enjoying the food. Florence was happy to know the truth behind her stay here, and that brightened her mood even more. At least there'd be no secrets here.

Whatever Chef Auguste had whipped up to Virginia's dismay must have been either chucked at the last minute or saved for the *pièce de résistance*.

So when the man rolled out an elaborate cart topped with something hidden under a polished silver cloche, Florence gulped.

"Mademoiselle, I welcome you to the household with the warmest regards! Tonight I have prepared for you a dessert of the worthiest of my efforts. A true delicacy that will delight and capture your senses!" She thought for sure he'd twirl his curled mustache for added effect.

With a flick of the wrist he revealed a very unusual-looking tart of some sort, or at least that's what Florence thought it was until an odor hit her.

The smell he unleashed from whatever was in the pie tin was like a good punch in the kisser, and the only thing she could compare it to was the stench of a honey-covered fish on a plate. A honey-covered *dead* fish on a plate. She wasn't at all surprised to see the small bowl of what looked like tartar sauce placed between her and Aunt Julia.

If she wasn't careful, her eyes would start watering worse than when she was chopping onions. And what a sight that would've been!

Aunt Julia, calm and poised as ever, dabbed at her nose with a handkerchief. "What's in this delightful delicacy of yours, Auguste?" she asked conversationally.

Chef wiggled his eyebrows in the kind of smug manner that reminded Florence of a villain in one of those Charlie Chaplin films. "It is pickled fish organs in a honey-breaded tart. Fresh from the fish market just this morning! I ordered some of the finest clover honey from upstate for this very occasion. Does it please, madam?"

Aunt Julia gave a soft sigh. "Oh, Auguste. This is such a lovely dish, I do regret to see it ruined. But you see, as delicious as the delicacy most certainly is, I'm afraid I've found that the nature of fish organs does not sit well with my digestives and I couldn't in good conscience eat any. I'm so very pleased by the kindness that went into your meal, however."

Chef's face fell. "But of course, madame. I would never wish to cause you illness. Perhaps mademoiselle, you wish to try?"

Still in shock over her aunt's obvious but smooth lie, it took Florence a moment to realize he was talking to her. The hint of hope in his voice almost cracked her.

"Of course, Chef. I-I'd love to. I'm not... familiar with such an exotic dish." It was not as easy for Florence to lie, but she didn't want to suffer the dessert's *consequences* either. "Except, I'm very sensitive to fish innards myself as well. It must be a family malady, you see. The rest of dinner was marvelous though, and I also appreciate your warm welcome." Her wavering smile didn't compare to her aunt's benign manner, and Chef sighed and dropped his shoulders.

"I do not want such a thing for you, either. As you wish, my ladies. I will return to the kitchen. I am most certain that Hamish or Virginia might appreciate a nice slice of the tart after they have finished their duties for the night."

There was no mistaking the startled cough coming from the corner where Hamish was standing.

Chef retreated to the kitchen and Hamish quickly followed suit, leaving the two women at the long dinner table sharing a knowing look.

Aunt Julia reached over and placed her hand atop Florence's. "My apologies, dear. I didn't wish to put you on the spot like that. Auguste's tastes can be a little more varied than most and I wasn't sure I wanted to go through another episode like last week."

Florence tilted her head to one side. "What happened last week?"

There was a pinching of Aunt Julia's lips that told her she was trying to stifle a smile. "I dare not recall it as a lady. But I will say that I was indisposed for quite some time after a particularly slimy cut of what he called *calamari*."

"I've never heard of it, but slimy doesn't sound very appetizing at all."

"It wasn't, to be truthful. Ah well, he does urge us to try new things and at that he is very helpful." She glanced past Florene to the clock. "I'll be retiring for the evening now. If you require any extra linens, ring the buzzer and let Virginia know."

With another pat, she stood up and left the dining room with a trace of Chanel No. 5 wafting behind her. In the back of Florence's mind she thought of the samples she and

Bernice had tried at the J. C. Penney in Akron. Why, it wouldn't surprise her if Aunt Julia was friends with Coco Chanel!

And what was even more astounding than the thought of brushing shoulders with the chic designer from Paris was that, even with the commanding nature Aunt Julia held, it was truly something to behold a good dose of wit in her.

Well, there was nothing left to do but go back to her rooms for the night. At least until she had a better understanding of how the household ran, she wasn't exactly sure she was welcome to wander around late at night.

Florence got up and picked up her plate, ready to take it into the kitchen, when she realized that Aunt Julia had left hers where she sat. How odd it was not to go wash up the dishes after dinner, but maybe that was how things were here. She ended up leaving her plate too, feeling strangely about it.

Heading up the dark and polished stairs, she was lost in thought somewhere between the second and third floors until she went to take another step and screeched. The fat orange cat had bounded down the stairs and collided right into her before yowling in a mad dash to get away. Florence pressed her hand to her chest, breathing heavy. She wasn't used to possible animal encounters around every corner, but she'd most certainly be more careful about it from now on.

THE COOL, silky sheets were bunched up at her feet, but Florence still felt too hot.

She rolled over to face the other side, squeezing her eyes shut. The radiator beside the bed worked a little too well and now, despite the chilly temperature outside the row house, she was dying of thirst.

With a sigh, she resigned herself to getting up for a glass of water. Mother always swore that warm milk did the trick, but all it ever did for Florence was make her wish she had a slice of cinnamon bread and butter to go with it.

Even with the lights flipped on in the lavatory, she couldn't seem to find a glass for water. She debated bending her head down to sip the water as one did from a drinking fountain, but the style of the faucet made it near impossible.

"Oh, come on," she muttered to herself, fumbling for the lights again. Her throat was so dry there was no ignoring the thirst, which only meant one thing—she would have to venture downstairs into the kitchen.

Pulling on her yellow satin negligee, she found her matching pair of quilted bedroom slippers and an oil lamp by the radio and headed out the door, taking very careful steps. Luckily the home was newer and didn't have the same creaky steps her house in Ohio did.

The lamp's dim light was the only one she encountered all the way into the dining room. With the home entirely in electricity there was no need to keep lamps burning, and she swallowed hard against her dry throat as she crept into the room she saw the chef and Hamish walk into earlier.

It was a rather large butler pantry with another door leading into yet another smaller pantry, this one to hold the bags of grains and flours and such. A door opposite finally led into the dark kitchen.

It was hard to see much in the kitchen, but she could tell that it was much larger than the one back home. She passed by what looked like one of those new electric iceboxes, taller than her, and very quietly started going through glass-inlaid cabinets to try to find a glass to drink from.

She grabbed the plainest one she and poured herself some water, grateful for both the cool air in the kitchen and the cool water, though it tasted a little funny.

Washing and drying the glass on a nearby dish towel, she headed back out into the dining room and then the grand hall and up the steps, relieved that she hadn't accidentally run into anyone, or any furry animal for that matter. It was entirely too late in the night for a scare like that.

It was also too late in the night for visitors, though apparently someone hadn't gotten the message.

She froze at the second floor landing, leaning her ear toward the direction of voices coming from the right. It was hard to make out the rest of the long hallway but she could see the bright light spilling out from underneath one door. It was just barely cracked so she couldn't see a thing, but she could hear some of what was going on.

From the sound of it, there was a handful of women inside the room. Papers were being shuffled about, but other than that, Florence had no idea what they were doing.

Coming from the opposite end of the hallway was that sneaky cat's face all aglow as it crouched by the open door. The cat, unaware of her presence, pawed at the door until it was just able to slip inside to the affection of everyone inside.

"Oh, you wretched thing. Coming to spy, are you?" A girlish voice chuckled loudest over the others.

"Please do keep it down, Viv. I'm certain the rest of the house would like to sleep through the night," a more familiar voice scolded quietly as familiar black skirts swished past the crack of the door. "Do we need to move the meeting elsewhere?"

Aunt Julia. What in the world was Aunt Julia doing hosting others in the dead of night? She didn't seem the sort who would be up to such a thing, and as far as Florence could tell, this wasn't some sort of urgent occasion.

A couple of women giggled but were quickly shushed. The door shut abruptly and Florence stumbled, startled. Did she dare creep closer to listen? She chewed her bottom lip, frowning. She prided herself on not being a snoop in someone else's business... but then again, had she not snooped around in Mother's writing desk in the first place, she might've never ended up here.

"That was different," she said softly enough to herself that no one would hear. Maybe she'd carefully wheedle it out of Aunt Julia in the morning over breakfast.

Whatever the case, she wasn't sure her aunt would appreciate her sneaking around like that cat, so she wound her way up the stairs, her head full of more questions than she could fathom the answers for.

4

October 14, 1925

Even with an entire other room filled with chic clothing, shoes, and accessories to explore, Florence was still puzzling out what she'd heard last night on the second floor. It wasn't any of her business, of course, and she wasn't one to pry, but it was admittedly odd for someone—especially someone like her aunt—to be entertaining guests in the middle of the night.

Was this something they did in elite society? Or as Mother put, the *highfalutin*? A fête that she wasn't aware of, perhaps? Maybe she should just mind her own particulars and explore the other parts of the house instead. There was plenty of that to do, most certainly.

"Well, in that case…" she said to herself, pulling open the door to the closet, "I'll just take a gander in here."

Her jaw dropped. How was it even possible to call this a closet?

It was like opening a door into a new world sparkling with the latest fashion. A pendant light hung overhead in the middle of the room, bathing everything in a cheery glow, revealing row after row of clothes in more shades than a rainbow could count. Everything was separated by occasion. Pajamas and nightclothes, coats and heavy sweaters, day dresses, pleated skirts, capelets and shawls, and so many blouses!

Running her hand along the waterfall of genuine silk and chiffon evening frocks and gowns in the chicest styles she'd ever seen, she sighed. "Don't go pinching yourself now, old girl."

And the hats! Oh! Florence had never been gaga over shoes, but she did love a pretty hat. There were plenty of shoes to peruse as well, some in styles she'd only seen in magazines at the drug store.

At the very end, around the shallow corner, were the accessories to match the outfits. Belts and gloves, stockings, and a rack that held all sorts of different handbags and purses on full display.

"I don't know how, but I'll have to find a way to get you here, Bernie. You'd just love it," she said with a soft laugh to herself. After all, she had to share this treasure trove with *someone*.

There was even a tall bureau with all manner of undergarments for her to wear. Everything had been well-planned and thought of, and she couldn't imagine how long it must have taken for it all to be put together. She gathered up one of the nearby charmeuse blouses and held it up against her. It looked as though it would fit her perfectly. How had Aunt Julia known?

Of course—Aunt Julia must have simply asked for her measurements from Mother. Did she do the shopping herself, or did she have someone else choose it all? They were definitely not Aunt Julia's style, so she could only wonder.

After taking far too long to settle on a floral print pleated dress with an ivory bow at the collar, Florence nabbed a simple brown felt cloche hat with beaded pink flowers. There were so many shoes to choose from but she much preferred doing her walking about the house in her worn-in Oxfords. It didn't make sense to blister up her feet on her first full day in New York.

It was almost nine o'clock on the dot. There was a certain liberation in not having to get up with the sun any longer, though she wasn't sure what was expected from her. Aunt Julia's letter mentioned companionship and helping to run the household, but Florence didn't know whether that made her part of the help or not, though Aunt Julia had said she was not a servant. Florence glanced back toward the closet and over at the silver mirror reflecting the inquisitive look on her face. Something told her Virginia's room didn't look quite the same.

Curiosity sparked under her skin as she visited the other rooms on the fourth floor. There were three more guest rooms, considerably smaller than hers. And past the steps to the attic was a sewing room with yards of fabric laid out along a few tables, while the mannequin sporting nothing but a straw hat scared the stockings right off her. She shook her head before going down to the third floor.

Judging by the ornately carved heavy pair of doors shut off from the rest of the place, this was Aunt Julia's floor.

She continued down to the second floor, pleased to see there was a wealth of rooms to examine. The same floor where she'd seen and heard her aunt last night was empty, but full of things with which to occupy her time with if she so chose.

The room that cat had sneaked into turned out to be a billiards room of all things, dark and masculine in its features and the only room along that hallway. Billiards tables took up much of the center of the room though there was a wide bar along one side as well as several smaller round tables and chairs dotting the rest of it. If Florence didn't know any better she would've thought she'd just walked into the sports pub down the street from the AT&T building.

She knew it was very nosy of her, but she wound her way past the tables and looked over the bar top. Not a drop of drink anywhere to be found, of course, just empty glasses drying on the rack. She raised an eyebrow, the corner of her mouth quirking up.

Interesting.

By the steps, there was a rounded bay window that overlooked the back property of the brownstone, and she could see Benny pulling Aunt Julia's car into the carriage house below.

The other side of the floor housed an office that appeared smaller than Uncle Albert's study downstairs and recently used. A music room was beside it with a shiny black grand piano, couches to lounge on, and both a gramophone and a stand-up radio to listen to. Florence smiled. Hopefully there were some good records to browse.

There was a powder room wallpapered in a cheerful blue-and-white print, and past that was a closed door that had dozens of books carved into the wood of it.

This must be the library! Her heart soared. If there was one place she could picture herself spending hours, it was a lavish library. Surely with the rest of the home, this was just as impressive.

She threw open the door with a wide grin, ready to take it all in at once.

5

Florence blinked.

It was the library, yes. There were large windows that let in plenty of sunshine, yes. But she was rather surprised to see the less extravagant layout of the room. There were built-in shelves along one wall at hardly half capacity, with two stuffed leather chairs and ottomans with a floor lamp between the pair of them.

And when she read the spines of the books, she was underwhelmed. Where was the fiction? Most of these were books on boring topics such as personal finance and, oh no... *The Manners Book*.

She shuddered. The amount of times she had to read from this particular book in her school days. The pages of it probably still sat in the bottom of Summit Lake from when she and Bernice had gleefully chucked their copies into it after graduation.

"What a boring old collection you turned out to be," she said with one hand on her hip. "Oh well. I'm certain I spotted a public library in walking distance. Maybe I'll get lucky and they'll have the latest Christie novel."

Back down to the main level, she glanced around the corner behind the grand staircase and saw Virginia placing folded linens in a closet.

"Good morning," she called out, wincing when Virginia let out a squeak of surprise. "Sorry, I didn't mean to sneak up on you like that."

Virginia waved her off. "It's no trouble. I'm just not used to someone being around back here. Hamish is out running errands and the missus is out as well. Were you needing something, Miss?"

Florence gave her a knowing look. "Please, call me Florence. And no, I was just looking around the house, getting my bearings straight."

She nodded. "Of course. Well, if you'll be needing breakfast, I can whip up something for you. Auguste isn't in for another hour, as your aunt likes a late breakfast herself."

Truth be told, Florence wasn't opposed to eating but her curiosity pulled at her, wanting to keep looking around. "That's all right. I do appreciate it, but maybe I'll just wait until she eats. That would give me a chance to speak some more with her."

Virginia gave her a quick curtsy. "As you wish."

"Wait. I'm sorry, I know you're busy," Florence said with a smile, "but really, there's no need for the curtsying and all."

"It's just standard practice, but I suppose as you're the guest, if you prefer it that way then that's fine by me. Only I wouldn't want to offend the missus."

Florence hadn't thought of that. "I see. Well, if it's of any consequence perhaps we can learn to be friends and you can just call me Florence without the curtsying the same as any other friend would. I daresay I'll need someone to show me how this place works as it is."

But the housemaid raised an auburn eyebrow at her in surprise. "Friends?"

Florence's own cheeks burned. She didn't think it would be an issue but maybe she had misstepped with the idea. "If that would suit you, I mean. If not, that's all right too. You are very busy here, I'm sure, so if that is too much to ask then we can pretend I didn't say a word."

"No, it's not that. I'm just...your aunt doesn't have many in the way of long-stay guests, much less new residents coming through here, and since my husband James and I live downstairs, we don't see many others." Her bright green eyes searched Florence's as her mouth drew up into the perfect cupid's-bow smile. "What I mean to say is that it's a kind offer and I will gladly take you up on it."

Florence let out a long breath, laughing. "What a relief! I thought I'd really stuck my foot in it this time."

"Not at all, Miss—er, Florence," Virginia recovered, hoisting a stack of kitchen linens into her arms.

Winking, she let Virginia get back to her duties, and set out to explore the rest of the main floor. The dining room led into not the kitchen but a smaller breakfast room, as well as separately into a butler pantry that fed into the main pantry and finally into the large kitchen. This was the maze she'd miraculously stumbled through last night to get her drink of water.

Past the reception room on the opposite end of the house was the parlor room, leading out to the sun porch. The walls of windows in the conservatory next door to it warmed up the room considerably, and she smiled as she strolled around to look at all of the different flowers and plants. Papa would've loved this room, as much as he loved being outside. Maybe it was a trait he shared with his older sister.

Speaking of outside... the sunlight spearing through the glass room put Florence in the mind of taking a nice walk. With a quick stop back upstairs for her coat, she slipped her hands into her pockets and pulled on her leather gloves, stepping out into the brisk air.

Autumn was skittering orange and yellow dry leaves and kicking up a whirl of dust from the road as one car passed her by. The weather wasn't too different from mid-October in Ohio but it was certainly windier.

She decided to go down the way they'd come in yesterday, interested in whether the library was open or not. Luckily for her it was, and it housed an exceptional array of all sorts of books in many different sections. She'd snatched up the first copy of *The Secret of Chimneys*, eager to get started on it tonight in bed. There was something about a good mystery that left Florence flipping through the pages late into the evening.

Perhaps that was why she couldn't seem to get the scene of the cracked door to the billiards room out of her mind. She scolded herself. Making mountains out of molehills once again!

Two borrowed books and a brand new library card later, she was pleased to return down St. Luke's Place with her arms full.

By the time she'd closed in on Aunt Julia's row house, a car had pulled up alongside the sidewalk and, moments later, two women emerged.

Aunt Julia fixed her ride-along scarf, untying it to reveal a perfectly kept updo. Thanking the driver, she cast an amused glance at the other woman. "She'd do well to remember what happened last time she hosted the Ladies Christmas Luncheon. How am I to handle both her dramatics and our next NWP meeting?"

Her companion's tinkling laugh reminded Florence of something.

It struck her as odd that the stranger's voice was familiar to her but she was sure she'd heard it before somewhere. Somewhere recently...

Her eyes went wide as it clicked into place. This was one of the women she heard last night in the billiards room with Aunt Julia! Funny, that.

The other woman patted her hat down with a soft groan. "She's a terror, she is. Getting her pearls in a twist like that over the dessert menu. If I weren't the upstanding lady I am, I'd invite Adelaide to take a swing at me just to knock her flat on her large caboose!"

"Honestly, Vivian. I don't need you squabbling with her, either." Aunt Julia sighed, catching Florence walking toward them from the corner of her eye. She cleared her throat in quite an obvious manner that made Florence feel as if she'd been dropped neatly into a conversation she wasn't invited to.

Vivian's kohl-lined eyes batted in her direction. "Oh my word, do excuse me."

Florence didn't miss a beat. "Whatever for? Dessert menus must be held to high esteem no matter the occasion. Doubly so for anything with strawberries."

The other woman flipped her pashmina scarf over her shoulder with an appraising look. "And what about mint?"

"Debatable."

That earned her another girlish giggle. "She'll do nicely, this one," she said as she shielded her eyes from the sky and swung toward Aunt Julia. Her tone was brighter than the sun shimmering against the glass pane behind her. "Wherever did you find her, Julia?"

Aunt Julia pressed her lips together in a firm line that suggested a tempering of her thoughts. Florence had been studying these tiny details about her aunt in the moments where nothing was being said.

"My niece, Miss Florence Winters. She's my brother's youngest daughter, in fact, and she's come to live with me." Aunt Julia gestured a gloved hand in her direction. "Florence, this is Mrs. Vivian Laurie. She's a neighbor of ours."

Mrs. Laurie's wide smile grew even wider. "How lovely to meet you, Florence. I'm—*we're* at Number Fifteen, at the south end. My husband, Gerald, and I."

Florence couldn't help but find Vivian Laurie's less formal friendliness with her aunt both amusing and intriguing. Everything about Julia Bryant was strong and refined and having a neighbor so open as Mrs. Laurie was quite the contrast. Something about her made it seem like a dalliance at a friend's in the middle of the night wasn't out of the ordinary.

She politely offered her hand, though the question of what the ladies had gotten up to last night in the billiards room was still hovering around like an annoying gnat in her head. "Pleasure to meet you, Mrs. Laurie," she said, gazing down the south end of the street. "I was just taking a walk and admiring how lovely your neighborhood is."

She beamed. "We were one of the last families to buy in. It really is the picture of exquisiteness, is it not? It's precisely why I told Gerald we mustn't dillydally and go straight to the bank the very day I walked along this street. He's a smart man, he is. He was leaning more toward Agnes Street, but I told him this was it. I simply couldn't see myself anywhere else. And he did what any good husband does."

"Oh. What does a good husband do? I wouldn't know myself, much to my mother's concern."

Mrs. Laurie let out a peal of laughter as she clutched her mink-lined coat to her chest. "Darling, do not tell a soul that I've said this to you," she said in a conspiratorial whisper dramatic enough to rival the *Tales of the Dark Hour* radio show, "but you are not missing out." She gave a wink that matched Florence's smile and they both giggled.

Aunt Julia wasn't so impressed, and the giggling quickly died off.

Mrs. Laurie straightened up, pulling herself to her full height, which was not saying much considering her petite stature. Even in the thick coat and heavy-skirted black dress, it was easy to see that. "Once it was all said and done—*men's business*, as he called it—he handed me the checkbook and pen and left me to it. I spent the first year handpicking everything from the draperies to the beautiful bone china set I had imported from England. Edward is a peach, he truly is. He made my dreams of running such a comfortable household come true and I will forever be thankful for that. I'd venture the same for you, Julia."

Florence remembered when Papa and Mama had attended Uncle Albert's funeral, which was an extravagant affair for a man who helped shape the city. That was five years ago and she hadn't heard a peep about him since, other than Virginia mentioning his study.

Aunt Julia fumbled with the scarf in her hands and bowed her head slightly. "Albert put us in a position to make the changes so desperately needed around here," she said softly. "From his hard work comes the ability to do what must be done."

Florence raised a brow. *Do what must be done?* What an odd thing to say! What could she have been talking about?

Her confusion only stuck more when Aunt Julia's expression returned to its neutral and polite way. "Have you eaten?"

Florence shook her head.

"Ah, I see. We've had our breakfast out this morning, but I'll see to it that Virginia prepares you something. Anyhow, Mrs. Laurie is here to help me plan for the Lions Club's annual Ladies Christmas Luncheon. We have quite a bit of scheduling to attend to," she said, gesturing for Mrs. Laurie to follow her.

The disappointment sprung up on Florence from out of nowhere. She'd hoped to talk more with her aunt, but if she was busy then there was nothing to be done. "I appreciate it, Aunt Julia."

Mrs. Laurie waved her fingers at Florence with another cheeky wink. "Too-da-loo, darling!" The pair of them headed inside and Florence stood beside the hedges, perplexed.

Do what must be done... it was still sitting squarely in her mind. What was it that must be done, exactly? It was said in an almost foreboding way and she couldn't shake the feeling that there was much more behind the words.

Florence tapped her fingers along the book spines, frowning. "I wonder if Virginia might know something about it," she said softly, eyeing the front door.

"Do you always talk to yourself like that?"

Florence's books went flying out of her arms with a jolt, thudding to the ground at her feet. Perhaps it was the universe getting her back for startling Virginia earlier.

Or perhaps it was just the younger blonde woman in the raglan-sleeved wraparound coat and chartreuse cloche behind her. "I'm sorry?" Florence dipped to pick the books up in a hurry.

"Oh, I've opened my piehole and really done it again. Sorry about the books," the other woman replied with a dramatic sigh. "You look new and I didn't know if you were lost, the way you were talking to yourself."

"You didn't see me speaking to Mrs. Bryant and Mrs. Laurie?" Surely she would know them if she was familiar with the neighborhood.

Her cheeks blushed even more under the rouge. "I did, but I thought maybe Dame Bryant was just asking you to leave the premises. I wouldn't really put it past her."

"My aunt doesn't hold a title like that." At least she didn't think so... "And why would she ask me to leave?"

Satisfied with a quick glance around, the woman shrugged. "She doesn't like people snooping. Wait," she said, narrowing her golden brown eyes. "The dame's your aunt?"

"Mrs. Bryant is, yes," Florence corrected her. "I'm living with her now."

"So you're the one Mama was talking about, huh? My mother is a member of the Parks and Socials Society with her, before you ask," the woman interrupted her in a clipped and girlish accent, patting the hat down on top of her dark blonde bob. "She mentioned something about a relative coming to stay with her at the last salon Mama made me attend with her."

Florence clutched the books tighter to her chest, curious. "Was that all she said?"

"Your auntie isn't exactly forthcoming. But either way, welcome to the neighborhood..." She gave her an expectant look, waiting.

"Florence. Florence Winters. And you are...?"

"Bitsy Parnell. I live back this way at number 2," she said as she jutted her thumb behind her. "Still at home. Perpetually and tragically single, I'm afraid." She held up her gloved hand as if she was showing off the vacant spot on her ring finger. "I'm looking under every bush and hedge for the right guy to fall madly in love with me, but no one has ticked all the boxes, you know?"

Bitsy sure was an open book. Florence would never dream of telling someone she'd just met about how woefully inept she'd felt in the romance department. "Ticked all the boxes?"

"I have a list, of course. Tall, dreamy, a member of the Elm Square Men's Club so I can get in without losing my father's membership, willing to take me out to the theater whenever I want, and from old money so I don't have to explain myself more than I care to," Bitsy said with a shrug. "Some may think I'm picky, but I prefer to call it having high standards. Besides, I couldn't very well bring some old schmuck with me to ladies night at the Cotton Club, now could I?"

The name rang a bell, but Florence knew next to nothing about nightclubs. She wasn't really the dancing type. "Well, at least you know what you like. Which would make it easier to know when you find it, I imagine."

Bitsy flashed an appreciative smile. "See? I knew I'd like you. You're not from around here—like a shiny new tennis bracelet! Though I'm sure they'll add you to the social register soon enough…the rest of the neighborhood is duller than a flat tire, so maybe you'll liven the place up some! It's lousy with the older lot, not a single eligible bachelor in the mix. They're all either married or out of the house." Her smile turned to a sour pout.

Florence was still trying to wrap her head around being considered a shiny new tennis bracelet when a thought struck her. Bitsy Parnell was sure to be chock-full of neighborhood gossip. And if she wanted to find the real dirt on St. Luke's Place, she was willing to bet Bitsy had it in spades.

"Then I suppose they're missing out," Florence finally said, the gears in her mind turning.

"And how!" That seemed to cheer her right up. "Say, why don't we meet up tomorrow? Do you have any plans, Flo?" She slipped her arm underneath Florence's, linking them.

Florence winced, hoping Bitsy didn't try to make *Flo* stick. The only one she let it slide with was Bernice. "None at the moment. What did you have in mind?"

"Well, I know for a fact that there's a demo tomorrow at Montgomery Ward's and practically all of the women will be there. Boring," she said, pretending to yawn. "But Mama is dragging me along anyway. Perhaps we could meet up there! I'm sure the dame is going."

"You keep calling her that... why?"

"Sorry," Bitsy said, covering the rising giggle. "It's just a name some people use. She's very, what's the word? Regal? Almost like she's been titled by the queen, you know what I mean?" She pushed her sleeve up to reveal a diamond-encrusted Rolex watch. "Oh fiddlesticks, I better get going. I didn't realize I was late for my singing lesson. I'll ring you in the morning!"

She squeezed Florence's arm and practically skipped away with a spring in her step. Perhaps it was a good thing Bitsy lived on the opposite side of the street and down some. Florence wasn't sure she'd want to be serenaded by her singing lessons any time soon.

She blew a stray strand of long hair from her face, still clutching her books. Tomorrow she'd try and drill Bitsy for some information on the street and perhaps even what to expect now that she was stepping into a new class of people.

And it might have been a bit on the nose, but who better to tease the idea of a late-night secret meeting than an obvious gossip? If anyone had a clue about what might have been going on in the billiards room, it would be Bitsy. Virginia was awfully quick to shut down the very idea, and she didn't want to put her in an awkward position by asking her.

But for now, she was ready to curl up with a good book and a cup full of hot tea in her room.

6

October 15, 1925

The morning pressed against Florence's eyes in a dutiful way as she sat up, struggling to remember where she was for a moment. It was still an odd thing to wake up somewhere completely new after her whole life spent in the same small house with her family.

The knock at her door had her clutching her sheets to her chest. "Yes?"

"Sorry, Miss. Ah, Florence, I mean. I've brought you up some breakfast!" Virginia's cheerful voice called out through the door.

Breakfast in her room? She glanced over at the small linen-covered table in the sitting room. Its presence finally made sense now that she thought about it. "Come in!"

The doorknob rattled as Virginia turned it carefully, the tray of food balanced in one hand. "I didn't mean to startle you, if I did."

Florence waved her off. "No, it's fine. I was just getting up. I didn't realize I'd be in for such a treat this morning," she said, gesturing to the tray that Virginia had set down on the small table. She nabbed her dressing gown from the upholstered bench at the end of the bed and wrapped it around herself.

"Mrs. Bryant usually has breakfast downstairs but she's up particularly early and wanted me to make sure you were up too. I thought what better way to soften the blow than with some homemade biscuits and preserves?" She was already spreading what looked like strawberry preserves across the biscuits, the scent of the buttery bread hooking Florence into her seat.

"That's so kind of you! You didn't have to go through all the trouble of it," she said as she took a bite. Her eyes fluttered as she savored the bite. Not necessary but wholly appreciated. "I don't suppose you'd like some as well?"

Virginia bit her bottom lip. "I'm not sure I should."

"Nonsense, it's not as if Hamish is going to peek around the corner," Florence laughed. The image of it had both of the women shaking their heads with matching grins.

"If you say so," Virginia finally said, sitting down in the other chair. "I haven't had anything to eat yet, myself. And Auguste's biscuits are to die for, truly."

Florence knew exactly what she meant. Mother's biscuits weren't bad, but they paled in comparison to the golden flaky bread in her hand. "Truly."

The two of them chatted for a few minutes over delicious food and even hot herbal tea. Florence uncovered a few things about the housemaid—she and her husband were newlyweds, she'd lived and worked here in the house since she was thirteen when Aunt Julia was kind enough to take her and her mother in after her father died in the war, she was an awfully good listener and an even better storyteller. When Florence pointed it out, Virginia had proudly claimed it was because of her parents. The Irish were well-known for weaving words into pictures.

"I have to admit I know nothing about the way life works here in New York City," Florence said with a sigh, finishing up the last of her delicious tea. It was a shame Mother wasn't a fan because she'd been missing out.

"Not many know the ins and outs of the society people's lives here." Virginia shrugged. "Unless you're in with the crowd, that is. Or if you happen to be paying attention in the kitchens." There was a sly smile on her face that led Florence to believe that her new friend wasn't as docile as she first appeared.

"I'm late to watering the plants in the conservatory downstairs. But I thank you for the sit-down. I'm not sure what your aunt would think of it, though," Virginia said wistfully, twisting a bit of her red hair back under her cotton headband.

"Think nothing of it. At the very least we can claim my ignorance at how to be a lady in high society. Mother certainly didn't prepare me for it." She smiled, the idea of her taking part in such a group still unnerving. But something stood straight up in Florence's mind so quickly she nearly sputtered out, "Wait! I nearly forgot. There's something I wanted to ask you about, actually."

Virginia raised a brow at her. "Yes?"

Florence leaned forward. "I didn't want to mention it before, but I noticed something odd the other night when I went to fetch a glass of water."

Right away Virginia tensed as if she were bracing herself for something.

"In the billiards room, I believe, was Aunt Julia having a party? In the middle of the night? I wasn't sure of the time, but it must have been nearly two or three in the morning." It occurred to her that Virginia very well knew if someone went through the hassle of cleaning the glasses that had obviously been used. What they were full of was anyone's guess, but Florence had a feeling it wasn't water.

The kindness that Virginia had shown Florence felt stiff, like she'd been extra starched after washing. "Mrs. Bryant keeps her entertaining to herself, you see, though I daresay you must have been having quite a good sleepwalking if you managed to find your way through the kitchens and back up the stairs again!" The laugh was a little too late.

Huh. Florence hadn't been expecting that kind of answer from her, but she supposed it was a housemaid's duty to keep her mistress's affairs private. At the very least, she was loyal to Aunt Julia, and Florence thought she might not get as many answers as she would've liked from her.

She smiled at her all the same. "Thank you for the food and the talk, Ginny dear."

The housemaid looked at her thoughtfully, smoothing down the front of her apron as she stood. "Ginny…" the word came slowly as she was trying it on for size. "I like it. Is there anything else you need?"

"No, I'm fine, thank you. I suppose I'll have to fish out something from that terribly tiny closet." She grinned. "Actually, Ginny, do you happen to know who furnished this whole room? And the closet? For the life of me I can't quite picture Aunt Julia being the one responsible for it."

Ginny scooped up the tray and drained teacups, her freckled cheeks bright red. "Well... Mrs. Bryant asked for some input when spiffing up the room for your stay. I may have mentioned *Harper's Bazaar* as a place to explore for a more modern look, seeing as you're my age. Not that I would know much about fashion," she said, gesturing to her uniform and sturdy work shoes. "I love the look of Mrs. Bryant's home and it fits her well, but something told me it would be better received if this room looked more like, well, *this*. It's one of my favorite places in the house actually. If you don't mind me saying so."

Florence's jaw dropped. "Then I have you to thank for this beautiful scene. I love it, I absolutely do. You've got a good eye. It puts my room back home to shame, I must say."

Tucking a curl behind her ear, Ginny shrugged. "James and I count ourselves lucky that our own room is cheerful despite the lack of windows. Your aunt is very kind in that respect. And as far as the terribly tiny closet over there," she said with that sly smile, "the missus had a fashion designer friend of hers come over and fill the place up. Her name escapes me... something French. Oh! Jeanne Lanvin, I believe."

"Jeanne Lanvin? Now I know I've heard of that name before. It just sounds stylish, doesn't it?" Florence pretended to tip a hat to the woman. "Thank you for the glad rags, Mrs. Lanvin."

THE DEMO WAS SET to start at the Montgomery Ward's opening hour, nine o'clock, so Florence quickly put together what she thought was an appropriate outfit under her crimson coat and found herself standing on the sidewalk with Aunt Julia as Benny pulled the car around.

"How are you liking your new clothing, dear?" Aunt Julia asked, straightening the gauzy but thick scarf around her hat. She'd explained how necessary it was for her to wear it in the car to avoid resembling a woodland creature when she arrived wherever she was going.

"It's all lovely. And I am so appreciative for the generosity. I hadn't realized living with you would come with so many... perks."

"You're very welcome, of course. Being a part of this household, your status will carry weight in town. We must ensure you look the part as well." Her studying gaze swept up and down Florence in an instant. "Word travels like lightning around here, so I'm sure it won't be long before everyone knows who you are. Not to worry, dear." She patted Florence's arm with her chamois glove-covered hand. "You'll become accustomed to it soon enough."

Florence had a hard time believing that one.

Benny pulled the sky-blue vehicle around, hopping out at once to pull open the door for them. "Good morning, Miss Winters," he said with a nod, pointing to the fleece blanket behind the seat. "It's pretty brisk out here today so you might want to bundle up back there. You don't want to mess up your pretty coat."

Her cheeks went pink but not from the cold. "I'll keep that in mind. Thank you, Benny." She did exactly that, smiling as he helped Aunt Julia into the back of the car next to her.

The engine roared to life and they were off, the chill from the morning's temperatures making Florence wish she'd thought to bring a scarf for around her neck, too. She wouldn't get caught out in this weather without it again, at least.

The store's wide sign marked the corner of the city block, where Benny dropped the pair of them off before going to park somewhere. Florence wondered where exactly he went off to, but Aunt Julia pointed for her to follow the signs in the store pointing to where the demo was being held.

There were so many people! Florence thought she'd seen crowded department stores before around Christmastime, but the group of women pushing their way to the front of the household items section was a crowd of its own.

Even more jarring, the fact that the women seemed to part like the Red Sea did for Moses as Aunt Julia stepped into their midst. Their gaze soon followed Florence as she tried to keep from dropping her head in her aunt's wake. Her mention of *looking the part* was still tumbling around in Florence's brain.

"Hello," she said politely, nodding to a few of the women toward the front who very clearly knew Aunt Julia as she sidled up next to them.

"What have we missed?" Aunt Julia asked mildly, unwinding the scarf from around her head.

"Nothing dear, you're right on time as usual," said a woman in a taupe broadcloth coat with over-the-top fur trimming.

She sported a pair of large ruby drop earrings with tiny diamonds twinkling all around them as she graciously lifted a shoulder, leaning toward Aunt Julia. "I had heard that Adelaide would be stopping by. She mentioned it yesterday evening when Harley and I were seated near her and Edward."

Aunt Julia gave a stiff nod and looked as if she were going to answer, but a gentleman in navy-blue trousers and a matching homburg swept into the scene with a wide and charming smile on his face. "Welcome, ladies of our great city! I am Franklin Peachtree, and I'll tell you what I'm here for. You. Yes, you heard that correctly, ladies. I'm here for you, to help you with the heavy load of housework that befalls your dainty shoulders. Or for many of you, your staff's shoulders," he said in a staged whisper. Some of the women around Florence and her aunt tittered and chuckled, though neither of them did.

Mr. Peachtree stepped out of the way, gesturing to the platform and built-up wall covered in red crushed velvet with large signs reading today's modern woman! and electric convenience! Two ladies in flowy tea dresses and elbow-length satin gloves walked around from the back wearing easy smiles. Florence had to stifle the laugh that threatened. These showboaters were very much professionals.

"We have for you today an array of modern household appliances that I and my assistants will demonstrate, starting with... the all-new latest model of electric washing machine for your laundering needs!" The women stood on either side of the clunky-looking metal machine, running their hands along its sides.

Already Florence was bored. Perhaps Anna and Mother would enjoy something like this, but Florence wasn't exactly thrilled at the new-fashioned ways to do the same old chores. When the washing machine would dry and fold the clothes and linens in question, that's when she would pay attention.

Behind her, a couple of women whispered to one another loudly enough that it was difficult not to overhear them.

"We should've been here sooner. Now we're stuck behind everyone else and I can hardly see over anyone. Being petite just doesn't serve me well in these types of situations," one of the women said with a soft sigh. Her tone carried a feeling of one who might blow away in the breeze if it blew hard enough.

The other woman was quiet for a moment. "I'm sure Julia wouldn't mind if you—"

"Nonsense, Mary-Ann. Now shush. I must pay attention. Our staff at Farringway House will need good notes from me in order to know exactly what I want," the woman who was not Mary-Ann said in a quick whisper. "And step away a bit, would you? That horrid wool scarf of yours is making my skin itch. Don't get caught out in the rain with it or you'll smell like Marty after a run-in with the hose."

Florence gritted her teeth. She wasn't nosy enough to turn around and get a good look at the two of them, but she also wasn't a fan of listening to them whispering right behind her.

Apparently Aunt Julia felt the same. She turned and looked at them over her shoulder, her steely eyes narrowed while Florence stared ahead. "Will you two please keep your comments to yourselves? Perhaps comment upon your poor cousin's appearance in private rather than for everyone else to hear, Adelaide."

She couldn't see them but she could practically feel Adelaide's stunned silence as Aunt Julia turned back to listen to Mr. Peachtree go on about the water pressure in the machine.

Behind them, one of the women whom Florence was certain must have been Adelaide, let out a harrumph.

The first demonstration seemed to drag on forever, but when Mr. Peachtree announced that the state-of-the-art washing machine was on sale now and available for order, that was the cue for everyone to either crowd him with their checkbooks out or disperse into the rest of the store.

"Well if it isn't the Ladies Group president herself."

Aunt Julia's smile faded as she turned away from a couple of women she'd just introduced to Florence. Fixing a politely neutral expression on her face, she tucked her handbag up under her arm. "And the vice president as well. Adelaide. Mary-Ann. Enjoying the demonstration?" She sniffled a bit, her nostrils flaring as she dabbed at her nose with a handkerchief from her pocket.

The woman whom Florence knew must have been Mary-Ann with the scarf nodded. "It's fascinating to see what they come up with nowadays!"

The other woman, however, pursed her coral-red lips together. "I found it dreadfully dull myself, but I possess more of an imaginative mind." She shrugged, her hand-painted red bangles clinking together as she smiled an overly sweet smile. Her movie-star looks struck Florence as something she used intentionally. "Had it been a play or perhaps a fantastical book, I might be more obliged to enjoy it. I'm only here to note to our staff at Farringway House how—"

"I see. Well, the rest of us who are feet-down on the earth have other things to tend to. Such as planning our lovely Ladies Christmas Luncheon," Aunt Julia interrupted, clearly meaning to halt the conversation. "My word, I nearly forgot to introduce you to my niece. Florence, this is Mrs. Adelaide Ramsey and Mrs. Mary-Ann Elmhurst. Adelaide, Mary-Ann, this is my niece, Miss Florence Winters. She's just moved into Number Seven with me."

Adelaide smiled graciously with a slow bow of her head. "Lovely to meet you, Miss Winters. How are you finding the place?"

Florence blinked. For some reason she felt compelled to choose her words wisely here. "It's a dream. My aunt has spared no expense in welcoming me to the big city, and I'm excited to see more of it."

This seemed to please Aunt Julia as she took her hand and squeezed it lightly. "I am glad to know you are enjoying your stay, dear."

Something about what she'd said must have set Adelaide into a mood. "Yes, she has a propensity for doing that, doesn't she?"

Florence couldn't help but stare at the pair of them as they narrowed their eyes at one another. What kind of bad blood could there possibly be between them? And yet... Adelaide had mentioned something about reading.

"Are you a reader too, then?" she asked Adelaide, hoping Aunt Julia wouldn't disown her for her curiosity.

Adelaide gave her a simpering look before turning her attention to Florence. "Oh yes. You see, men seem to think a well-read woman is a dangerous one," she said with a flourish of the wrist, running her now bare hand over the mink fur-lined collar of her coat. "I think it's wise to stay ahead of that. Would you agree?"

Florence chose her words carefully again. "I could see why they would feel threatened. I think a full library is the first step toward independence for anyone, but especially a woman."

Aunt Julia's eyes flickered over to her, and Florence felt the weight of judgment being made on her words.

"Well, my dove, you are certainly welcome to my extensive collection any time you'd like. I hardly have the time to read them all myself."

"Oh, that is such a kind offer, Mrs. Ramsey. Are you nearby St. Luke's Place?" Florence asked, hopeful that she was. The public library was wonderful, but she had a secret desire to see what kind of library a wealthy person like Adelaide Ramsey would keep in her home.

Adelaide's honeyed smile widened, her coral-red lips thinning. "We are not far. Merely eight blocks, I'd say. Though I drive wherever I need to go, so I could be wrong." She shrugged. "Ring me when you desire to visit. Julia has my phone number as it's on the social register of course."

Florence smiled. "Thank you. I will certainly keep your offer in mind." She gave a quick curtsy, unsure of what else to do. "It was a pleasure meeting you. And you as well, Mrs. Elmhurst."

Mary-Ann nodded, though she didn't hold quite the same delicate way about her as her cousin. She threw the wooly yellow scarf over her shoulder to keep it from covering half of her face. "You too, Miss Winters. Are you ready, Adelaide?"

Adelaide regarded her coolly. "I suppose. I know you're rather anxious to get back home. Which is precisely why you should learn to drive as I have." They stared at each other for a moment before Mary-Ann looked away. "Goodbye, ladies. We'll see each other at the next Ladies Group meeting, I'm sure."

It wasn't until they were standing off to the side of the next demonstration when Aunt Julia crossed her arms. "That woman is her own worst enemy, I swear it."

The last thing Florence expected was that Aunt Julia would bring up the obvious tension between her and Adelaide. And while she wasn't one to gossip, Florence figured the more she knew about the company Aunt Julia kept, the better.

"How so?" she asked lightly, slipping her gloves back over her cold fingers.

As if she only just realized she'd said anything out loud, Aunt Julia blinked, shaking her head. "It's nothing, dear. She just knows how to push one's buttons is all. Oh look! I daresay Miss Parnell is waiting for you to notice her back there." She nodded her head somewhere past Florence.

Sure enough, Bitsy Parnell gave Florence an exuberant wave as she turned to see. "That's right. We'd planned to meet up together here. Would that be all right with you?"

Aunt Julia smiled ever so slightly. "Of course. You are free to do as you wish, Florence. As long as you are back by a reasonable hour being out on your own, of course."

She thanked her aunt before winding her way through the rest of the crowd and to Bitsy. Arriving at Bitsy's side, she couldn't help but notice Adelaide Ramsey staring daggers in Aunt Julia's direction as she breezed through the revolving glass doors.

Whatever had happened between them must have been some tiff. Florence couldn't help but wonder if maybe it had something to do with the secret meeting she'd accidentally spied her first night in town.

7

THE REST of the morning went surprisingly well.

Bitsy, though she was chatty and sometimes woefully ignorant about how life worked outside of New York City's high society, was pleasant enough to walk with as they went about. Florence knew there would be a sort of disconnect between them, being how she was raised on a tailor's wages while Bitsy was unaware of the fact that people even existed outside her opulent life. But she also knew that getting along with the friends and neighbors of her aunt was expected of her.

And at least Bitsy knew the area like the back of her hand.

She'd gone on about everything from her dream wedding to not wanting children as they were *too much of a hassle*, up to her thoughts on the best places to shop around town. Something she'd confessed was a *delicious habit* of hers.

It reminded Florence of how much she was already missing Bernice and how she'd need to get on with penning her first letter to her best friend tonight.

Bitsy's favorite café was just down the street from Montgomery Ward, so they'd strolled right inside and sat in a cozy spot toward the back that Bitsy had proclaimed was the best seat in the house.

"Deedee's is fabulous, I tell ya," she'd said over a sweet cream coffee. "And clean as a whistle, too. You'd never know Old Nick was her brother."

Florence had raised an eyebrow. It seemed it would take a meeting or two before Bitsy realized she had no idea who any of these people were that she was talking so candidly about. "Is that so?" she'd said with a sip of her new favorite drink, something called an India Assam black tea.

"Oh applesauce! I'm just sitting here yapping away and you don't know a thing about it. I'm sorry, Flo. I get carried away sometimes." Bitsy had leaned forward, dropping her voice to a whisper. "Old Nick Colombo—he's the guy. He owns Nicky Caboodles, the best jazz joint outside the Cotton Club. Well, he owns a lot more than that place, if you catch my drift."

The wiggle of her thin eyebrows told Florence that this Old Nick guy wasn't someone you'd want to cross. "Hmm."

Bitsy had waved her off with a cheerful grin. "But that's just hearsay and I'm not one to gossip. How's the tea?"

Florence had met that grin with one of her own. "It's Florence, dear. And the tea's *delicious*."

❦

The morning lazily dipped into the afternoon and Florence decided that chatting with Bitsy was enough socializing to last her through the rest of the day and then some, so she nipped the library copy of *The Secret of Chimneys* from her room and perched on the comfortable bay window seat overlooking the carriage house. Clouds were rolling in and she did not want to get caught in a rain shower if she'd read outside somewhere. She'd save that treat for another day.

She turned a page, savoring the smell of the fresh print that had never been read before, when something caught her eye. Up the stairs stalked the orange cat, its tail flicking from side to side. It regarded her from the top step where it came to a stop.

Florence couldn't help but smile. "There you are. I was wondering where you'd run off to. I haven't seen you around." Never having a pet before, she wasn't sure if it was considered normal to talk to the cat, but it felt quite natural to her.

The cat's eyes seemed to narrow at her as if she were a dubious suspect in one of Christie's mysteries. Florence fixed a stare to match, though she ended up cracking a smile in the end.

"You're probably wondering why I'm here. I'd tell you, but I'm still a little murky on the explanation myself. Your owner—my aunt, that is—wanted me to find my purpose here, I suppose. I thought I was doing that back home but now I'm coming to realize that maybe I wasn't. Though I'm not sure what I am to be doing," she paused, catching her breath. "But I'm sure talking to a cat is *not* part of it."

She swung her legs down to make space for the cat, beckoning for it to take a seat. But it did not and instead continued up to the third floor without a backwards glance.

What a fickle little thing! She shook her head with a sigh and leaned back, wondering if the freedom to do whatever she pleased wasn't somehow softening her in the mind.

Later, at dinner, Florence brought up the cat and received a fitting answer.

"Oh, him," Aunt Julia had smiled as she cut into her mincemeat pie. "That's Sneaky."

"He does seem very sneaky, yes," Florence had agreed.

"His name is Sneaky. He's every bit a feline without a drop of shame in him." Aunt Julia's mouth had quirked up a bit.

Sneaky. What a name for a cat! It was hard not to smile at the thought of it.

She had to admit it was nice getting to know Aunt Julia. There was an air about her that really did feel regal, as Bitsy had put it. Eating dinner with her was a special occasion, and Florence was sorry for it when dinner was over with.

She knew it was pointless but she spoke up anyway, still unaccustomed to leaving her dirty dishes on the table. "Should I help with these? I feel strange not helping out somehow."

Aunt Julia, to Florence's surprise, did not admonish her. Instead, she folded the napkin in her lap and gently placed it on the table, and set her silverware on the mostly empty plate. "I will say this; you are not required to do so as that is what I pay my staff to do. They are being paid well for their hard work and are happy to do it. You, on the other hand, are a resident here now, and I am paying them to also handle your affairs as needed. I will not tell you no despite it being the proper thing to do, but perhaps you should ask how they feel about it. You might be surprised with their answers."

Florence considered this. "I will do just that. But Auntie... sorry, Aunt Julia, you mentioned something this morning that I was also wondering about. Forgive me for sounding so uninformed on the matter, but you said it was important to look the part in representing your family. I don't claim to be completely unaware of what you mean by that, but could you perhaps elaborate so I don't, well, make a fool of myself?" It was an awfully forthright thing to bring up and she felt somewhat naked by doing so. Her aunt was a powerful woman but Florence had the feeling that she was also a good woman deeper than that.

Aunt Julia stood up and folded her hands in front of her black-and-gold bolero-styled evening dress from years past. "You are observant as ever, my dearest niece, and that assures me even more that it was a good choice in requesting your presence. It is true, there is an expectation of my name, Bryant. My husband's legacy continues in his companies and the community work I find it is my duty to oversee. The city would not be as it is without him, and daresay us. People will come to know that you are my kin, and they will associate you with all of this," she said, gesturing to the stunning room around them. "I ask that you continue to be the generous young woman that you are, and not make trouble for me. You are an adult and I gather you'd know what constitutes trouble—anything that would cause others to look down upon our good name, as it is. I know I can expect that of you without any issue."

Florence nodded. "Absolutely," she said, deciding to head through the pantries and into the kitchen.

"And Florence?"

She turned back around. "Yes?"

The sly smile was so quick to flicker across Aunt Julia's face that Florence thought she imagined it. "I don't mind it if you consider me your auntie."

And with that, she carried herself elegantly out of the room.

Florence pretended to salute her and grinned. Perhaps this really was just the beginning of the rest of her life. With a woman like Aunt Julia helping guide her, she was sure to accomplish something... wasn't she?

🐚

AT FIRST SHE thought she'd left the radio on, but a few slow blinks and fumbling around in the dark woke her and she knew that wasn't it. There were no radio shows or music of any sort in the middle of the night unless you counted the static's hissing.

Then she heard it again. Footsteps.

She froze on the spot, waiting. Her next few steps were already spinning around in her mind. She'd slip into her house slippers and grab the coat rack... no, something smaller... the book maybe? No, too small. The oil lamp! She'd grab the oil lamp and sneak over to the....

More footsteps softly sounded outside the door. Were they outside the door, or were they somewhere else? Florence quickly dashed whatever idea was brewing in her head and grabbed her kimono, wrapped it tightly around herself, and crept closer to the door with the oil lamp held high.

She listened closely. The footsteps didn't sound like they were necessarily on the fourth floor, though it would've made sense seeing as the guest rooms were up here. But it was nearly one o'clock in the morning! Who was busy moving into a guest room at this hour?

They were farther away than that. With a sigh, she looked over at her slippers tucked against her bed. She couldn't very well go back to sleep with someone possibly rummaging around or even worse.

"No sense in being a child about this now, old girl," she said to herself quietly, resigning to putting on her shoes and lighting her lamp. Except the lamp was out of oil and didn't seem to want to light.

"Rats! How am I supposed to see now?" She considered the match but that would only last for a few moments before it burned down. She'd have to go investigating in the dark, in this enormous house with who knew how many nooks and crannies?

With a gulp, she turned the doorknob, thankful when it didn't rattle and alert anyone. She paused in her doorway, listening.

More footsteps; these were not coming from down the hall or even on the fourth floor at all. They were barely audible, which told her they must have been on a lower level. She peeked over the edge of the landing, unable to see much of anything.

She was going to have to go down the stairs.

It bothered her that she didn't have any oil in her lamp to see but at least she had it, well, just in case. Though she didn't want to think of the scenario in which it would be needed. She very carefully picked her way down the steps, hoping to avoid any creaking.

The third floor she knew was Aunt Julia's and her heart thumped heavily in her chest when she heard the footsteps even louder. But there was nowhere for them to be. There was only the landing and, to the right of it, her aunt's quarters. To the left of the staircase was nothing. Just a wall.

Yet she was sure she could hear the footsteps and even some movement getting closer. Biting her lip, she continued down to the next floor.

Now she was nearly to the third floor landing where earlier she'd been sitting at the bay window, reading. The full moon's light shone through the window as she crept closer to it, its shimmer saturating the carriage house and trees below.

She paused to see if she could hear anything else. And when she heard voices, she clapped one hand to her mouth.

Voices? Where were they coming from? The unwelcome fear of the dark settled into her bones as she pressed herself against the wall. The fear whispered *ghosts, spirits, a haunting*, but she shook those silly thoughts free.

The voices had to belong to real people somewhere in this house, that much she knew. And Hamish and Ginny, well, maybe they were just running behind with their duties. Perhaps they were working late and she was skulking around in dark corners like a ninny for absolutely no reason.

The main staircase was heavy with footsteps coming up from the grand foyer and Florence couldn't move an inch even if she wanted to. All she could do was hope it was Hamish with his surly attitude, ready to lay into her for startling him.

But the moonlight pouring in from outside said otherwise.

She watched, her eyes wide as the outline of a woman in a heavy fur coat emerged onto the second floor's landing. Florence looked closer, trying to find something to help her identify this lady as it most certainly was not Ginny in her simple housemaid's uniform.

And she bit back a gasp when the woman gave a startled cry, bending down for a moment until she popped back up with a laugh.

"Such a wretched thing. You really know how to scare someone, don't you?" the girlish voice crooned. The answering meow earned another laugh. "Let's go. We have work to do, you know," the woman said before continuing down the one side of the hallway, which led to the billiards room.

Without thinking, Florence hiked up her kimono's soft hem and quietly clambered down to the landing to peek around the corner. Sure enough, the crack of light that spilled through the billiards room's doorframe illuminated the pretty face of Mrs. Vivian Laurie as she entered without shutting the door behind herself.

Florence waited a beat, still unsure, but followed her, inching close enough to peer into the room. There was a quiet noise that sounded like a latch opening, but what confused her the most was that she heard no sign of anyone in the room. Not even Mrs. Laurie.

It wasn't like the last time she came across this strange late-night gathering, and when she finally found the guts to push open the door, she was gobsmacked.

No one was in the room.

Not Aunt Julia, or Mrs. Laurie, or even Sneaky the cat. It was as if Mrs. Laurie had vanished into thin air.

Whatever was happening here was most certainly out of the ordinary, and Florence knew without a doubt that there would be no returning to bed without finding more answers. She wanted the truth and had hoped that Aunt Julia would be a sensible person and give it to her.

Even still, she didn't want to be caught trying to find those answers. She walked over to the bar and looked over it and then around it, but no one was there. She even had the funny notion of checking for a trapdoor underneath the floor here, just like she'd read about in the news where bar owners had turned their now defunct businesses into illegal alcohol-laden establishments they called speakeasies. It sounded like something from a novel or from a film even, but she was only a little disappointed to report that the floor was hiding nothing but dust bunnies.

With a sigh, she walked back around the room in search of... well, she wasn't sure quite yet. The room didn't exactly lend itself to many hiding spaces, and she couldn't picture anyone slipping up underneath the pool tables either.

She placed her free hand on her hip, frowning. Where could she have gone?

The heavy clunking sound of booted footsteps startled her into nearly upending the oil lamp, and she rushed out of the room, keeping a close eye on it just to see what happened next. Hopefully no one else was on their way up the main staircase.

Florence couldn't believe her eyes. Part of the far wall between a pair of stuffed armchairs popped open, and out came Ginny, still in her housemaid uniform, carrying a tray full of emptied drinks. Ginny didn't seem to notice the door to the room was more open than it should've been, thankfully, and she set to work washing up the glasses in the barkeep's sink, humming something softly to herself.

Florence stared in awe. A secret room! Secret meetings at all hours of the night and now this? What exactly was Aunt Julia up to?

When Ginny finished up, she dried her hands and headed back through the strange opening in the wall, the door of it clicking quietly back into place.

Was she going to follow Ginny? Florence bit her lip as she took several steps back into the room. There was no denying it, she was too curious.

But how? She gently placed her hand on the same part of the wall that had come open, her mind working overtime. Ginny hadn't used a key so there must have been another way inside.

She pushed gently on the door and it popped open to her surprise. Not wanting to lose her nerve, Florence set her oil lamp down on the nearby table and peered around the door into the dark.

There was a steep set of narrow steps leading up, and she noticed at the top the warm light of another room. From what she could see and hear from the bottom of the stairs, there were more women in Ginny's company. Though she had no clue how many or what they were doing.

Only one way to find out.

She dropped down to her hands and knees, wincing at the dusty old steps as she crawled up them. When she got to one of the last few, she paused in the shadow.

From here she could just make out some of the faces of the women. Most of the women were seated at a long table that reminded her of the drafting table her father used at the tailor shop to create patterns.

There was Mrs. Laurie of course and not surprisingly Aunt Julia, but there were also a couple of the ladies Florence had been introduced to this morning at the demo, mixed in with unfamiliar faces. Ginny performed rounds of tidying up where surfaces were stacked with odds and ends like books, papers, and what looked like maps.

In fact, there was a large map of the state of New York behind Aunt Julia who sat at the head of the table, her fingers splayed together like a church steeple in front of her.

"We will forgive Vivian her tardiness," Aunt Julia said in a somewhat wily manner.

The rest of the ladies tittered, and Mrs. Laurie shrugged good-naturedly. "What can I say, darling? They don't call it fashionably late for nothing."

Aunt Julia rolled her eyes but not in the stern way Mother did with Florence. "I've heard from Alice this morning while at the demo. She was in town to give a speech at Barnard College. She had quite some news on the ERA front. Sarah dear, are you ready to take down the minutes?"

One of the younger women held up a fountain pen before dipping it in ink. "Ready, Julia."

Florence propped her head up a bit more, trying to see if she could get a little closer. Who was Alice? And what was the ERA front? It was all so terribly intriguing that she couldn't bear to pull back now. Part of her was irritated with the fact that perhaps she didn't have the best understanding of her aunt, but the larger part of her was more curious than ever about what was really going on under her nose.

An orange tail swished past the top step, and staring down at her in the same untrusting manner was Sneaky. Florence held her finger up to her lip, fervently shaking her head as if that would make a difference to him.

He sat back on his haunches, still staring.

She stared back.

He let out a loud yowling that immediately ceased the moment every lady in the room turned her attention toward him.

8

"What is he...? Is that...?"

"Someone's there, Julia!"

"But who could know?"

Everyone stood at once and Florence nearly banged her head, trying to skitter back down the steps.

Aunt Julia appeared in the doorway, the light of the room outlining her as an avenging angel. She looked down the steps at Florence with an unreadable expression in her eyes while Sneaky's tail flicked this way and that beside her.

"Stay put. I will be down momentarily."

Everything in Florence told her to bolt, though it didn't make sense. She'd been spotted, and despite whatever reason Aunt Julia had for hiding these meetings—which Florence concluded must have happened regularly—she didn't feel like she was in trouble.

But then again, she hadn't suspected Aunt Julia was holding secret meetings in secret passageways that led up to secret rooms, so what did she know?

There was hushed whispering met with Aunt Julia's calm voice. "I will handle it. Please continue on without me."

Florence backed out of the narrow passage that led to the steps, watching her aunt slowly descend them. She licked her suddenly dry lips.

There was a silent moment where perhaps Aunt Julia was waiting for her to speak, but when she didn't, Aunt Julia sighed. Clasping her hands together out in front of her, she seemed even taller to Florence.

"You have many questions, I am sure. But as I am currently in the middle of... certain affairs, I will have to speak with you on it in the morning."

That was not the answer Florence was expecting. Nor was it one she was willing to accept just yet.

"I'd like to know what's going on. I know this isn't the first time those women have been here in the middle of the night. The other night I went to find a glass for water downstairs and happened to see you all in here," she said, pointing to the floor. Well, there was the truth of it. She was on thin ice, she felt, but it was too late to turn back now.

Aunt Julia tilted her chin up and looked down at Florence. "Is that so? You didn't mention it to anyone?"

This time Florence bit back her initial reply, searching for the right way to answer. She had mentioned it to Ginny but she did not wish to get Ginny in any sort of trouble. "I tried to convince myself it was an odd one-off party that maybe dwindled down later than it was meant to." Of course this wasn't necessarily true, as she'd thought it was much stranger than that.

"As I've said, we will speak on it in the morning. You should go back to bed." Aunt Julia meant it as a way to steer Florence out the door but she stood up straighter to meet the look in her aunt's eyes.

"You requested my presence here so that you could maybe help me in some fashion, yet you are keeping things from me in the same breath. I don't think it's out of line for me to question what's going on now that I live here."

It was as though there was a trench in the dirt between them and Florence had gained some high ground. She swallowed against the rising lump in her throat. Had she thrown this whole opportunity away just to argue with Aunt Julia?

Aunt Julia turned and picked up the oil lamp Florence had completely forgotten about, handing it to her. But when Florence went to take it, the elder woman paused. "I understand your frustrations. Please trust that I would not put you in any sort of compromised situation without your knowledge. Now, that having been said, this whole thing can be better explained in the morning after we've had a chance to wake up and take some tea. I can come up to your room myself and speak with you, if you would like."

Another more mature woman might have talked down to Florence as if she were a child to be bribed into bed early, but not Aunt Julia. She spoke more as an equal than her superior.

Even still, Florence knew she was being placated. She sighed and took the lamp in her hands. "All right. When should I expect you?"

"It will be a late night. Let's say nine thirty in the morning, then. I'll make sure to have Virginia bring up what we need. See to it that you find your way back to your room." She glanced down at the empty lamp she'd just given her and went to retrieve a new one from the bar top, lighting the wick in the lamp before handing it over to her. "This might help."

Florence nodded and realized Aunt Julia was waiting for her to leave before heading back up the passageway's steps. Who knew if she'd lock the door behind her?

She took the lamp and made her way back up to the fourth floor, only to have fitful sleep until the morning.

※

OCTOBER 16, 1925

FLORENCE STARED through the steam rising up from her teacup, waiting for Aunt Julia to begin. She was on time, right at nine thirty, and admittedly Florence had only just managed to pull on her stockings and Oxfords when her aunt had come knocking.

Now it was very clear that she was finding ways to stall, which Florence couldn't help but find a little amusing. Julia Bryant didn't seem like someone who ever had need to stall. You could tell everything ebbed and flowed around her and that she almost always had things under control.

Seeing her stirring her tea around and around and staring down into her cup with such intention, Florence wanted to sit back and drum her fingers on the small tabletop out of impatience.

And then she began.

"When I first moved to Jackson Heights, I was newly married, just nineteen years old. The city was starting to come to life and I wished to be a part of that. Albert's business was becoming more successful and we found ourselves pulled into a new world full of possibilities. Forgive me for the introduction, dear..." she said in a faraway voice.

"With the new life came a new reality. I was suddenly surrounded by people on all sides, each of them wanting something from me. My story, my advice, my secrets, my money." She shook her head. "I made mistakes on who to trust with them, but I'm a quick study. But as Albert's business grew, we were put into a position of privilege that seemed to raise our stature higher and higher. I stood on the top of this pedestal only to realize that I was unhappy. Your father and I were not brought up in this kind of lavish lifestyle, as I'm sure you're aware."

Florence was very much aware. Papa's father was a farmer his whole life, and so was his mother. They'd both died before she was born, but she didn't know much else past that. Papa never wanted to talk about his parents or what life was like for him before he married Mother.

She nodded. "Papa's told me a little bit about it."

The sad smile crept up on Aunt Julia's face and just as quickly slipped away. "Our parents were good people. John is a man and men are not quick to speak on their feelings, let alone let themselves truly feel them."

It was easy for her to say, but Florence didn't necessarily agree with her. Papa felt things deeply. She believed it was one of her best qualities she'd inherited from him.

She cleared her throat in hopes that her aunt would get back to the story. It wasn't that she had anything better to do, but Florence was very curious and hated for them to get sidetracked now.

"All of this to say that I wanted purpose. I'd learned earlier that I was... unable to have children. Albert was crushed." Aunt Julia drew in a shuddering breath that caught Florence by surprise. "I couldn't do anything about it so I felt it was my duty to find a different purpose in life. If I couldn't contribute to society by raising well-mannered and kind people then I needed something else to busy myself with."

"This was right around the time I was visiting a friend in London. She'd invited me to a salon where a young woman was speaking about the British suffrage campaign. I wasn't a political theater kind of woman, but I thought if my friend found it interesting enough then I could accompany her and maybe meet some other interesting people." A new kind of coy look spread across Aunt Julia's face. "I thought myself dull in comparison to many of my friends who had such passions for things in ways I did not. But when I went to this salon and heard the young woman speak, something came over me. She was alive in a way that I was not, though I was wealthier than most people in the room."

"The way she spoke about women and our needs being pushed down since the beginning of time, well, those words moved me. I couldn't help but think of my mother who worked until her fingers bled but was never appreciated in the way my father was. I thought of the opportunities your father would have while I was relegated into marrying if I wanted to become a proper woman."

The silence in the room was tangible. Florence knew in that moment that Aunt Julia knew exactly how she felt, and the knowledge of that was something she was going to have to consider on her own later.

"But you did, didn't you? Become a proper woman, I mean," she said.

Aunt Julia nodded stiffly before taking a long sip from her teacup. "Yes, I did. And I do not regret a moment of it. But it did not fulfill me in every way and so I found what did. Working for others. Not in the way you're thinking, no, but in a way that would promote change from the ground up. The young woman at the salon went on to hand out pamphlets and I'd asked her if she needed help giving out more. Alice was more than willing to take me, a woman eight years her senior, under her wing to help out in ways others could not. She and I have been close ever since, and she's taught me quite a lot. One thing I learned on my own, though, was that this city needed us, needed *me*. So I have been making it my duty to see to it that I give the city what it needs. Whatever that may entail."

She knew her tea would go cold but Florence couldn't find it in her to bring the cup to her lips. She was too busy staring at the woman sitting across from her.

Aunt Julia had always seemed distant, like a character in a novel rather than her own family. But the truth was far different. She was living her own story the way she wanted it, and from that Florence was in awe of her.

"That is very admirable, Auntie. I can only hope to find the same kind of purpose in my life as you have. However, I don't quite understand what that has to do with the secret room and those late-night meetings with those other women. Are you just throwing parties?"

She was nearly shocked right out of her stockings when Aunt Julia boomed with laughter. "Oh, you are as straightforward as your father, are you not? You do remind me a lot of him." She dabbed at the corner of her smiling mouth with her napkin. "They are not parties but meetings. We are the Women as Equals Society, and we hold our meetings out of the public eye due to their nature and our places as the upstanding members of the city."

Florence thought of the few unfamiliar faces she'd seen from her corner of the steps last night. Women who wore plainer clothes and women who did not look like her or Aunt Julia.

She tapped her finger to her chin. "What does your society do, exactly? I saw maps."

"Observant as always. We keep maps for a variety of reasons but it helps to know where things are needed most. We work and live within the different boroughs of the city, and we use our resources and money and power where it's necessary. I continue to help fund two of the settlement houses in the city, for example."

"Keeping your meetings private... so that you can work from the inside?" Florence guessed. It was starting to come together in her mind. "I assume Virginia knows about it. Does Hamish?" She was getting nosy, for sure, but it was all so fascinating and she couldn't really imagine Hamish not knowing, but also it was difficult imagining him being sympathetic to the cause. All she could picture was him looking on with a scandalized twitch of his old-timey beard and mustache, overhearing what went on in the meetings.

"They do, yes. Virginia is invited to the meetings of course because she lives here and I believe it best to have an understanding from women at all levels in life, but she chooses to serve them even though she is off-duty. And Hamish..." She clucked her tongue in a disapproving way. "He is a traditional man who is set in his ways, but he also considers his loyalty one hundred percent to me and Albert's legacy. He would never speak ill of our society or break our trust."

"But he's not a... supporter," Florence finished. "I can't say I'm surprised. Oh!" she said, suddenly remembering someone else. "And Benny? Sorry, Benjamin?"

Aunt Julia finished her tea and placed her spoon across the top of the teacup. "He's not formally apprised of our understanding, but he is our driver when needed, even when it's late in the night. He's a smart lad; I'm sure he's put some things together. And again, I have his full loyalty and trust. I wouldn't expect him to throw that away."

That made sense to Florence. She could imagine Benny being the kind of guy you could trust, but maybe that was because he had a charming way about him.

"I will say one thing before I must go, however." Aunt Julia stood up, her expression slipping into something more serious. "It is most especially important that this does not get out to a few of my... acquaintances you may recall. Adelaide Ramsey and her cousin Mary-Ann Elmhurst, for starters. Mrs. Ramsey stirs up trouble wherever she goes and I believe she suspects something, though she may not know what that something is just yet."

Florence arched a brow at her.

"She's close with many others in my circle and I have reason to believe that she would think of our collective as something to use against me," she said. Her mouth formed a thin line, reminding Florence of a schoolteacher she did not want to cross.

"Then I will make sure to mind my *p's and q's* with her," Florence said with a quick nod. "Your secret is safe with me, Auntie."

Aunt Julia leaned forward and patted her shoulder. "I believe it. Thank you for listening, dear. I better be going now."

❦

The ink dripped and smeared on the page as Florence quickly remembered what she was doing and tapped her fountain pen into the ink well with a sigh. She'd been staring down at the pretty peach stationary from her writing desk for who knew how long.

This letter was supposed to be easy!

But every time she went to write the first words after *My dearest Bernice*, she drew a blank. It was hard to think of where to begin and she knew Bernice was waiting on her. Of course she could pick up the phone and call her—Aunt Julia most certainly could afford the long-distance phone call. But they'd agreed to be pen pals too, and here she was, unable to think of what to say.

If Bernice were here, she'd smack her with her handbag for being such a Dumb Dora.

The grandfather clock down the hallway chimed at five o'clock and Florence's stomach seemed to rumble in agreement. Dinner was still an hour away so she snagged one of the leftover biscuits from that morning and made sure not to drop any crumbs on the paper as she sat back down.

"Florence?" Ginny knocked quietly on her door.

"Come in," she said with a mouthful. She smiled and tried in vain to wipe the crumbs from her face as her new friend opened the door. But Florence's smile slipped away instantly. "What's wrong?"

Ginny's face was paler than normal, as if she'd seen a ghost. "There's been some trouble, I'm afraid." She rushed over to Florence, her red curls sticking out all around her in a cloud of auburn, and she patted them down to no avail. "Mrs. Laurie came by for lunch with your aunt but instead they were visited by the police."

The pen dropped out of Florence's hand and rolled across the paper leaving a dark, inky trail. "The police?" A heavy sense of dread filled her lungs. This could not mean anything good.

Ginny nodded. "They came to tell them that Mrs. Adelaide Ramsey has been reported missing by her husband. And..." She drew in a shaky breath, her big green eyes wide as saucers. "They think the missus has something to do with it."

9

Florence slowly rose from her seat at the writing desk. "I'm sorry, could you say that one more time?"

"Mr. Ramsey reported Mrs. Ramsey missing to the police first thing this morning, and they're downstairs now, speaking with Mrs. Bryant because they say they have cause to believe she may know of Mrs. Ramsey's whereabouts," Ginny repeated, slower this time, wringing her hands in her apron. "Your aunt asked that I come tell you she would be busy speaking with them in the reception room."

Which actually meant that Aunt Julia wanted Florence to know that something was going on without alerting the police to it. She went to Ginny and placed her hand on her shoulder, trying to calm her.

"I'm sure everything is all right. Perhaps they think since Aunt Julia saw her at the demo the other morning that she might be of some assistance."

But the other woman shook her head. "I don't think that's it, though. Detective Marshall implied Mr. Ramsey wants to speak with Mrs. Bryant in a way that... sounded as though he thinks she's the reason his wife is missing."

Florence frowned. "Well there must be some sort of misunderstanding there. Why on earth would he imply such a thing?"

"I'm not sure. But I came up here to let you know like she wanted. You don't think... you don't think they could arrest her, do you?" she asked, her green eyes round and misty. It was so very obvious she cared for Aunt Julia that a jolt of warmth shot through Florence's chest.

There was no need to worry poor Ginny any more than she already was, but Florence wasn't completely sure of how the law worked here in New York City. She didn't want to lie but at the same time, she knew things weren't quite the same as they were back in Ohio. At home, hardly anyone did anything to provoke an arrest, much less an upstanding woman in society.

"I doubt they would even if they wanted to. They'd have to have some way of proving Aunt Julia had something to do with it. And I hardly see how they could pull that off, seeing as she certainly would never become involved in criminal activity."

Ginny didn't look all that convinced but she nodded anyway. "Maybe."

Florence reassured her again before mentioning that Aunt Julia probably would want her nearby in case the detective needed anything. Ginny took off, just as spooked as she was when she'd come in.

Glancing down at the mess she'd made on her desk, Florence groaned. She tossed around the idea of going downstairs to listen in on whatever was going on but she decided she'd better not. Aunt Julia wouldn't be too pleased and, besides, she was an adult, *not* Pollyanna... no matter what they used to call her when she was a kid.

"Guess I'll have to write you later, Bernice," she said as she picked up the inkwell between two pinched fingers.

Washed up and red-faced from scrubbing at the ink from the desk, Florence found herself pacing around her room, her trusty Oxfords clunking heavily across the wood floorboards.

How long had it been since the police had arrived? Two hours? Three? Would Ginny come back up to let her know the news?

She did her best to keep her manicured nails out of her mouth. When she was nervous and not paying attention, she had a bad habit of biting them down to the quick. Mother's disapproving looks were usually there to help curb it, but not anymore.

The sunlight from the morning had already been covered in a gloomy gray, darkening her room as if it were much later in the day. Everything looked washed-out and colorless outside her window, and Florence threw on a warm sweater to keep the chills from roving up and down her arms again.

She glanced at the clock and away, glanced at it again, and sighed. This was ridiculous. She couldn't just be expected to sit up here with whatever was happening downstairs!

Perhaps if she went down for a different reason she might find whether the police had left. From her window she couldn't see the front street, only the back where the carriage house was.

Standing in front of her mirror, she smoothed down the front of the cream-colored sweater and nodded at her reflection. Her mind was made up—she was going downstairs to find out the truth whether Aunt Julia liked it or not. She couldn't imagine her being too upset about it, but she'd found very recently that you couldn't really tell people's motives just from speaking with them a few times.

So, when she met Ginny halfway down the staircase, she stopped short. "What happened? What did they say?" she asked, looking her over. Ginny didn't seem quite as distressed as before but she also didn't look at ease.

Ginny sighed. "They asked her to follow them to the police station and she asked if they would question her here instead. She didn't see the point in going all the way there when they could just ask whatever they wanted from her here. I don't think the detective liked that very much, but they ended up saying yes and she escorted them to the study."

Florence leaned forward expectantly. "And?"

"They've only just left. Mrs. Bryant has asked to be left alone for the evening. I can't say I blame her… they were in there for a while."

"Did she say anything to you about it? About what they asked her?" Florence tempered the impatience in her tone. She was just grateful that Ginny was there to relay things to her this way.

But Ginny shook her head. "Not really, no. She complained of a headache and asked if Hamish could bring her dinner."

Well, that wasn't going to be much help.

"All right. I suppose I should just wait to speak with her over breakfast. Imagine, being accused of such a thing. Do we know any more about when Mr. Ramsey found Adelaide missing? How long does one wait to figure out someone's missing and not just out late?" It was more of a rhetorical question, though Florence wouldn't mind Ginny's take on it.

Truth be told, she couldn't remember a time when someone had gone missing in Jebediah. Maybe when her neighbor Douglas had fallen asleep in the school's cellar on accident...

Ginny just shrugged. Was it Florence's imagination or did Ginny seem a little... off?

"Are you okay?" she asked, feeling badly about pestering the woman with so many questions. "I don't mean to be so nosy."

"No, no. If anyone is being nosy it's me." She glanced down at the stack of hand towels in her arms. "I may have listened in some when I was dusting in the dining room."

Florence wanted to smile out of sheer pride, but caught herself. This wasn't something to make light of. "Really? Were you able to hear anything?"

"It was hard to hear—those doors are solid. But the detective must have walked closer to the door because at one point I could hear him talking about a letter. They found one in Mrs. Ramsey's boudoir the same morning she went missing." Ginny gritted her teeth before looking past me and up the stairs. "It was a letter she was writing to someone, but they didn't know who. In it she'd written something about being afraid of the missus. That your aunt had it out for her and wouldn't stop until Mrs. Ramsey was silenced. Or at least that's what I think he said. He was quite loud."

A letter found in Adelaide's boudoir didn't sound like incriminating evidence against Aunt Julia. After all, they were just words and she had an alibi. Unless.

Unless Adelaide had been kidnapped in the middle of the night when Aunt Julia's alibi couldn't be verified without many lies and misdirections from everyone involved. Florence thought of the secret passageway through the billiards room and the Women as Equals Society. If Detective Marshall pressed too hard and actually searched Number Seven, was it possible they'd find the truth on the second floor? If they wanted incriminating evidence then they'd have it by the truckload there. It certainly wouldn't look good on Aunt Julia.

"This letter. They don't know who it was addressed to?" she finally asked.

"I don't think so, no."

"Hmm. I'm curious about who it was intended for. And why it was never sent."

Ginny put an apologetic smile on her freckled face. "I'm sorry, Florence, but I better get back to work. The last thing I need tonight is to be scolded by Hamish for not making sure everything is perfect for Mrs. Bryant in the morning. He gets so crabby when she's ill."

Florence moved aside. "Of course. Don't let me keep you."

She had some thinking to do as it was and smiled at her friend before continuing down the steps. Downstairs in the dining room, Florence walked over to the windows and looked out to the main street, watching a young woman pushing a baby stroller past.

Adelaide Ramsey may have been a rather disagreeable woman, but no one deserved this. No one deserved to be put up on the missing persons list hanging on the community board in the public library.

It made Florence shiver just to think of what kind of trouble a woman like Adelaide could be in at this moment. Had something happened to her? Had someone taken her? If they had, what was their motive? Someone as rich as Mr. Ramsey might have adversaries, as regretful as it would be. Or maybe she was just letting her imagination get carried away.

She still couldn't puzzle out how Aunt Julia had been tied up in the whole thing, though. Why would Adelaide name her in some sort of conspiracy? Mr. Ramsey was probably hysterical trying to find his wife, so he may have misinterpreted a conversation or something else. Surely he wouldn't actually believe in this letter or something as absurd as Julia Bryant kidnapping Adelaide. Or having someone *else* do it for that matter.

She clutched at her throat. What kind of city must this be, where someone could just disappear? She thought of the towering buildings and the side streets with so many shops and cars and horse-carts and even the streetcars.

There were a lot more places to hide in New York City.

October 18, 1925

Her fingers worked quickly, tugging the toggle clasps in place on her crimson wool coat. There were other coats of varying fabrics and warmth in the huge closet, but Florence was fond of this one. Besides, there was a beautiful navy cloche with a deep red cardinal embroidered along the side of it that perfectly matched the coat. She grabbed it and a pair of charcoal suede gloves and closed the closet door behind her, giving herself one good look-over before heading out the door.

Aunt Julia had requested breakfast in her room this morning—a missed chance for Florence to talk to her about last night. She didn't want to be too cross with her, especially given how lengthy had been the questioning of her aunt. Or was it an interrogation? Were the two things different? She wasn't sure and she didn't have time to pick up one of her Christie novels to check through.

Which left her with a plan, albeit a risky one.

While her aunt was dealing with her own worries, Florence needed to feel like she was doing something—anything—to help her. No one had called and no one had stopped by with any hopeful news on Adelaide Ramsey's whereabouts, which led her to believe she was still missing.

Thanks to Bitsy's mentioning the social register, she had the Ramsey address written down in her pocket, sure that she could find her way there.

She wasn't particularly clever with directions but Florence managed to find Dartmouth Street after picking up a free map from the library. The streets were laid out in a sort of grid system that made it easier to navigate, and four blocks down and two streets over she stood outside of the Ramsey home. A wrought iron gate bore an ornate 'F' that apparently stood for Farringway House, according to the sign under it.

For all the walking and time it took to get here, Florence was still unsure of what exactly she was going to do to get inside. The goal was to search for Adelaide's letter in her room, though she was aware that it could very well be in the police's hands. It was maybe even silly of her to come at all, but she felt like someone on Aunt Julia's side should take a better look at things, at least.

How to get it? Introducing herself to Mr. Ramsey as Aunt Julia's niece was out of the question, so what could she say instead?

She searched her mind for a good answer and nearly dropped the map when the front door opened. A man with oiled-back hair and a thin mustache regarded her with obvious suspicion. "Morning, Miss. May I be of assistance?"

Of course he was being careful—the mistress of the house had gone missing. And it hit Florence at once what to say.

She bit her lip, doing her best impression of when her mother was in her hysterics. With a sob, she brought her hand to her mouth, blinking back the tears that weren't there. "I'm so sorry to intrude on Mr. Ramsey. I was meant to visit with Mrs. Ramsey this morning in the library and only just heard." She sniffled for added oomph.

The look on the butler's face softened ever so slightly. "I see. And your name, Miss? Does Mr. Ramsey know Mrs. Ramsey was expecting you today?"

"Er, I'm not sure if he knows or not," she said, quickly thinking on her toes. "My aunt is a friend of hers from the, er, Ladies Luncheons?" It wasn't technically a full lie, though Aunt Julia was plenty clear on the fact that the two of them were not friends.

The butler nodded and opened the door wider to let her in from the cold. "Right this way, Miss. If you'd like to wait in the reception room, I believe Mr. Ramsey is in his study. I will let him know you are here, though I cannot guarantee he will be able to speak with you, given that he is busy working with the police to figure out what has happened with Mrs. Ramsey."

She made a show of dabbing at the corner of her eyes with a handkerchief from her coat pocket. "Of course, of course."

He was off, leaving her in the small room filled with crystals dripping from practically every surface. While Aunt Julia's place was timeless and elegant, Farringway House was an odd collective of the expensive. Things that didn't seem well-suited were heaped together in one room, clashing for attention. All for the sake of displaying wealth. It felt like it was a pretty near metaphor for the differences between both women.

A few minutes passed and still no Mr. Ramsey. When heavy footsteps fell outside the room, Florence straightened up in her seat.

A man in a burgundy suit walked right past the opened door without a look inside. She frowned and slouched back against the chair.

And then the man came back by, his eyes unfocused. "I'm sorry, Miss, but who are you and why are you in my home?"

Florence jerked herself upward at once. "Mr. Ramsey! I'm so sorry, I-I know you must be busy but I heard about Mrs. Ramsey and wanted to let you know that I... that I..." She searched for the right words. "Your wife wished me to come see your library. You see, we had a visit planned for today but I only just heard the terrible news." She decided against pulling out the extra stops. It was already bad enough that she was taking advantage of the butler, she didn't want to say too much to Mr. Ramsey in his frantic state.

He stared at her as if she were a book written in a foreign language. "The library? I hadn't realized…" Mr. Ramsey mopped at his glistening forehead. "Ah, quite right. Well if my Addy said you were welcome to the library then by all means take a crack at it. It's in the east wing, up those stairs behind you and to the right. They'll be the double doors midway down the corridor there. On the left, you can't miss them. Or should I have one of my staff assist you?"

"Oh, not at all," Florence said hastily before clearing her throat. "East wing, left down the corridor with the double doors. It shouldn't be much trouble."

He nodded. "As you wish. If you do need anything, please let one of the staff know. I'm sure you'll run into someone up there." With a quick tip of his bowler hat, Mr. Ramsey turned away from the doorway and left her there.

She took a moment to compose herself. That felt almost too easy.

The gleaming double staircases were made from pure marble and she gazed up at the landing above. She listened. It didn't seem like any of the staff were around after all. Even the butler seemed to have wandered off.

This might be her chance.

She hurried up the steps, careful not to trip. Following the directions, she found the library's immense set of double doors.

With a sweeping sense of déjà vu, she took a deep breath and pulled open the doors. The handles were thick and metal and cold in her hands, while the doors gave way with a groan.

If Aunt Julia's library was conservative then Adelaide's library was fit for a lavish castle, like the ones she'd read about in fantastical books. Inside was the largest and most spectacular library Florence had ever seen.

This was what she'd pictured when she imagined what kind of room would be awaiting her at Number Seven.

She very much wanted to sit and take it all in but she knew what she was really after, and with a heavy sigh, she closed the doors again. If someone had heard her then they would assume she was inside looking around.

Looking down the corridor both ways, she was relieved. None of the house staff was in sight, which was interesting considering how many Mrs. Ramsey had claimed were constantly bustling about the place. Whatever the case, she was free to explore the rest of the upper level. For now.

Much like Aunt Julia's place, Farringway House had multiple floors, but unlike it, the main bedroom quarters just happened to be on the same floor, only across the house in the west wing.

She drew in a deep breath when she found the second pair of double doors for the day. It was easy to guess that these might be the bedrooms with the modern styled entrance and mauve carpet beyond. She could just make out a sitting room and vanity from the crack of light between the doors.

"Please be empty," she whispered to herself.

And she stepped inside.

10

The bedroom quarters were equally separated with his on the left and hers on the right, while a large sitting room with a fireplace conjoined the two. Florence didn't have time to admire much of it so she crept to the right, her fingers crossed.

Adelaide's room was the picture of opulence. The walls were covered in deep purple draperies all around, pairing well with the mauve carpet and the collection of chandeliers practically dripping with swaths of crystal. And luckily for her, not a soul to be found.

She thanked her lucky stars and let out a breath of relief she hadn't even realized she'd been holding.

It was easy to spot the boudoir where a massive vanity stood that took up nearly half of one wall. There were dozens of beauty products in bottles and boxes, trays of accessories, and necklaces hanging from the corners of the mirrors. The light scent of jasmine tickled her nose as she took a closer look.

Whenever Florence had the chance to go to the movies with Bernice, their favorite films were always the ones with the damsel in distress. Not because she needed to be saved, but because she always had the most luxurious things. Aileen Pringle and Mary Pickford always looked so lovely. This room and this vanity reminded her very much of them.

There was also a desk on the wall opposite the vanity that she caught in its reflection. After scanning over the assortment of things neatly organized, rifling through the drawers, and checking on the floor all around the vanity, she was left empty-handed.

Maybe the desk, after all.

This was as cluttered as the vanity had been organized, with papers, books, a couple of maps, and a pair of reading glasses sitting atop a pile of papers.

What kind of work did Adelaide Ramsey get up to, anyhow? She sifted through the papers. Most of them were typed-up minutes from different meetings. It looked like she was on several community boards in key positions. *Secretary. Owner Trainer. Co-chair of Fundraising. Head of Charitable Events. Elite Sponsor.*

All of them painted a woman who was deep in the New York City elite, her influence spread across practically every avenue.

It was no wonder Aunt Julia grew tired of her—she must be around every corner!

There were also some lovely stationery samples stapled to what looked like a project she was handling for the Parks and Socials Society. One of the samples, a lavender color with gold embossing around the edges, had a sheet missing.

"If I were an overexaggerated letter, where would I be?" she wondered aloud, pursing her lips together as she flipped through more of the papers. The only letter she found there was addressed to Adelaide from an Elm Square Men's Club, thanking her for her generous donation.

She sighed. "Perhaps they took the letter after all. Oh, why did I come here to begin with?" She paused a moment to listen for anyone, making sure she wasn't drawing any attention to herself.

So far so good.

Adelaide had admitted to having a love for reading, hadn't she? It could've been something only Florence did, but sometimes when she wanted to hide notes or pictures or even a few spare dollars, she hid them in between pages in her books.

She took the first book from the small pile, *A Perilous Race*, and thumbed through it. Nothing.

The second book was thinner. A quick check and again, nothing was there. In fact, the next two books were empty too. She sighed as she grabbed the tattered book on the bottom and shook it out.

A piece of lavender paper floated out and fell to the floor like a feather drifting through the air. Florence gasped and snatched it up. Immediately Aunt Julia's name jumped out on the page to her, a page that looked like it might have been missing from the beginning of a letter. Indeed, a shabby '2' had been written in the bottom corner. Did the police only find the first page of the letter then?

She tapped her finger to her chin, following the words silently. The letter was written in what her mother would call chicken-scratch, all slants and sharp edges that blurred together in melted circles of dried splotches. Tears, if she had to guess.

...CAN YOU BELIEVE IT? That's three Ladies Christmas Luncheons in a row that I've been snubbed! It seems anyone in her path is just a pawn in her game. I'd like to step off the chessboard, myself. And I must say... and I say this in complete confidence, but I am sure that Julia Bryant is up to something. Something other than trying to shut me out of our circle of friends as I've mentioned. I don't know what kind of businesses she has her fingers in, but I doubt anything innocent or even lawful.

I grow tired of speculating but I grow even more leery of the woman. Am I being irrational? Please do write back.

Your darling,

A.

FLORENCE'S THROAT WENT DRY. So Aunt Julia had been right —Adelaide knew something was going on with her. She wasn't sure how she knew, it wasn't anywhere in this part of the letter, but Florence could only conclude that this part was not seen by the police.

Which was something to be thankful for.

For the life of her, she couldn't understand how one could get so spun up the way Adelaide had over Aunt Julia supposedly snubbing her somehow. This all sounded like the very same type of thing Mother and the other ladies at church dealt with. Silly, nonconsequential things that most certainly didn't lead to kidnapping.

"Why, this is just her airing her frustrations. There's nothing here that makes Aunt Julia look remotely responsible for whatever happened," she said softly to herself. Even the bit about Aunt Julia being up to something was just speculation by someone bitter toward her. It didn't mean much of anything.

Even still... Florence tucked the lavender piece of paper into her coat pocket, just in case. No one needed to pester her aunt any more than they already had.

Somewhat satisfied, she slipped out of the bedroom quarters and back down to the east wing, pretending to leave from the library. At the bottom of the steps she saw a maid curtsy before rushing out of the main foyer.

No one was there to see her out and she wasn't about to wait around and hope for someone to finally remember her, so she left as quietly as she could, the piece of paper feeling like a stolen secret tucked away.

The October wind brushed past her, trying to pull her hat along with it. She held the cloche down, annoyed but thankful she'd successfully pulled off her impromptu investigation.

Her pace was brisk as the weather but she wanted to put some steps between her and Farringway House and get back home quickly.

The surprisingly successful trip left her with the same remaining questions. Who did Adelaide write this letter to and why didn't she send it?

11

It was nearly impossible to concentrate on the roast duck and pasta on the plate in front of her. There were too many questions on Florence's mind as she slowly twirled her fork around linguine.

Aunt Julia had finally shown up for mealtime, albeit a little late, wearing deep brown wool skirts and a cream crepe de chine blouse fitted with a navy blue Dutch collar. Not a hair out of place, and a heavy cameo locket hanging between the bow collar, she was regal and untouchable.

Whatever her feelings about the interview nights before, her demeanor suggested she was beyond it, which made Florence apprehensive about bringing up the matter.

Before she'd even come downstairs, Florence knew she wouldn't tell her aunt about her little escapade at the Ramsey home earlier. She knew her behavior would be heavily frowned upon, and yes, understandably so. If it weren't for the fact that she was trying to prove Aunt Julia's innocence in such a nefarious thing, she would've scoffed at the very idea of sneaking into someone's bedroom and going through their belongings.

Then again, it'd been the only way Florence had forced answers out of her parents over Aunt Julia's invitation.

"Florence?"

She looked up to find Aunt Julia staring at her, slowly chewing her bite of food.

Straightening, Florence quickly brought her own bite of linguine up to her mouth. Her mind went reeling, grasping for the best way to broach the subject with her aunt.

"You seem rather preoccupied," Aunt Julia noted. She waited a beat. "Is anything the matter?"

Well, of course she was preoccupied! Florence smiled politely at her aunt and carefully placed her fork back down on the plate. "Actually, I do have a lot of things on my mind."

Avoiding the part about visiting the Ramseys, she asked Aunt Julia what the police had wanted, surprised when her aunt actually told her everything.

It had been an arduous ordeal for her, being brought up in a missing persons case. Detective Marshall had been patient with her and thankfully no one believed it was necessary to arrest her at this time. Especially once she'd phoned Mr. Dredd, her attorney.

Florence kept her thoughts on equating his name to his work to herself. "Were they even considering it? I can't imagine them having any kind of evidence to arrest you."

Aunt Julia, true to form, finished her bite quietly before answering. "There was a letter. Written by Adelaide, and all but pointing to me as someone who is capable of 'silencing her.' There was some mention about her feeling unsafe around me specifically. They took it as a sign to speak with me. And I told them that it is certainly confounding why she would say such things in the first place. I was honest with them about our relationship, I didn't want to tout us as friends, but that we were civil to one another and in many of the same circles and groups."

The names of some of the boards and groups Adelaide was a part of flitted through Florence's head. "So Mr. Dredd came by on your behalf?"

She nodded. "He did. We talked for a bit in another room before I told the detective I would do what I could to help the investigation, but that I was no longer open to questioning. They left soon after, though I'm not sure Detective Murray was too pleased about it. I know what he thinks of us, what he thinks of me." With a lift of her shoulder she sighed. "It can't be helped."

"What do you mean what he thinks of you?" Having the police against you certainly didn't make for a promising time.

"He's a man in power, Florence. He thinks lesser of me because I hold a similar power yet I'm a woman and I don't have a man in place to answer to. Or that's how he sees it, anyway. Detective Murray isn't a bad man—thankfully—but he does have his own biases. I have to work within the parameters given if I want to keep my name from being tarnished. *Our* name," she added, pointing between the pair of them.

Florence hadn't thought of that. "Does anyone else know?" She dropped her voice to a whisper, even though it was unnecessary.

"I'm not sure yet. I'll be open with the ladies at the next… meeting," she said, darting her gaze to the corner where Hamish was standing by. "But as far as anyone else, I can't possibly know. It is sure to have spread that the police were here, of course. We can only hope that no one knows what exactly they were here for."

For all of the freedom this kind of life gave someone like Julia Bryant, Florence couldn't help but wonder if there were different types of chains holding her down.

There was one more question she wondered. With a casual sip of her ice water she asked, "Do they know who the letter was to?" Maybe if she heard the first part then she might have a better idea of how the second part of the letter came into play.

Aunt Julia shook her head. "They aren't sure of it. It was simply addressed to '*Dear M.*' They're trying to figure it out. But certainly not anyone I can think of. With the exception of Meryl Ferris and Marjorie Desmond, I do not know who the mysterious M. might be. And those two ladies do not count themselves as close enough acquaintances of hers for such a candid letter as it was."

"Could it be Mary-Ann maybe?" Of course that didn't make any sense to her because she apparently saw her quite often. What would she need pen and paper for when she was so willing to gossip to her cousin right behind others?

She scraped at some of the pasta on her plate, wishing she could better enjoy such a delicious dinner. But there was just no joy in it for her tonight. Not when Aunt Julia's reputation was at such risk.

"No, I don't believe so. They would've surely checked in with her first," Aunt Julia said with a sigh.

"I won't speak ill of her but it does sound like she has it out for you, Auntie," she said, the letter in her room signaling her mind like a beacon. "Is that all it is, just her temperament toward you? She makes it sound like—like there's something more to it. An animosity of sorts. Did something happen between the two of you in the past?"

She could imagine some sort of tiff between two women in high society, though knowing her aunt, she couldn't see it as being something simple and catty. Aunt Julia wouldn't stand for such a thing, for starters.

But the corner of Aunt Julia's mouth quirked up into the beginning of a smile. "That's the funny thing of it. One would think we had some feud dating back long ago by the way she carries on. The truth is that I do not tolerate her attempts at coercing others. Because of that, she has concocted in her head this idea of me trying to rule over everyone. In reality, she is the one who is vying for control of everything in our circle. Or was." The amusement with the matter dissipated as she spoke. "I do hope she is all right, wherever she is. No matter what words or actions she's had against me, I don't wish anything bad upon her. This is all just so… so upsetting. The good detective is working on the case but if he's worrying about me, his mind is not where it ought to be."

Aunt Julia dabbed at the corner of her mouth with her napkin and placed it beside her plate before pushing away from the table. "That was a delicious meal. What do you think?" And just like that, the conversation had been closed.

With a nod, Florence took another bite of the duck, which had now gone cold. "Absolutely. I've only had roast duck once before and it was at Anna's wedding."

"Oh, lovely. I will pass it along to Chef." She glanced up at the large clock on the wall and pushed her seat back in just as prim and properly as she'd come. "We have church in the morning, as I'm sure you're aware. Trinity Church is a wonderful place. If you like beautiful architecture, you'll enjoy the cathedral. It's unparalleled, in my opinion."

Church was one of those things that Florence did for the sake of routine. Mother didn't like missing services, but usually Florence's mind was elsewhere. If it wasn't entirely looked down on, she would've much rather been reading a novel than listening to the pastor's monotonous sermon.

Though it was nice that Aunt Julia had noticed her love for architecture. "I'd love to see it."

And then a little thought wormed its way to the front of her mind, elbowing around until she blurted out, "Her cousin won't happen to be there at service in the morning, will she? Mrs. Elmhurst?"

Aunt Julia nodded, rubbing at her temple as if she'd grown tired of even thinking. "She will."

"Oh, good. I wanted to tell her how sorry I am for what's happening. I can't imagine this being easy for her. They seemed close." While Florence was telling the truth about wanting to speak with Mrs. Elmhurst, she thought calling Adelaide and her cousin close wasn't quite accurate. There was definitely some friction there at least.

"Of course. I am sure she will appreciate that." Aunt Julia shook her head. "Somehow it has slipped my mind to pay her a visit and see how she's doing with all of this. You're right. This cannot be easy for her and she and Adelaide are hardly ever seen apart." With a sigh, she smoothed down the front of her skirts and gave Florence a tired smile. "I'll be retiring for the night now. Truly," she said as if she anticipated Florence's questions about the secret Women as Equals Society meetings. "I shall see you in the morning, dear. The church service is at nine o'clock, so we'll need to leave here at eight in order to get our spots."

Florence gave a little wave. "Good night, Auntie. I'll see you in the morning."

Eight o'clock felt awfully early after this week of sleeping in until she saw fit, but it would allow her the opportunity to speak with Mary-Ann Elmhurst. If anyone had an idea of what might have happened to Adelaide, it would be her.

❦

OCTOBER 19, 1925

TRINITY CHURCH WAS JUST as beautiful as Aunt Julia had painted it to be. Unfortunately, Florence was not impressed by the length of the service. She did everything in her power not to yawn, but when the pastor had wished everyone a happy Sunday, she was glad to be up and moving again. Ginny and Hamish apparently attended another church closer to the house, and Florence found herself wishing Ginny was there to commiserate with.

"Ah, Julia! You're looking lovely as usual," an older man with a gold-tipped cane and thick, wiry eyebrows said as he approached the two of them on the way out of the chapel.

He went in for a more intimate hug but Aunt Julia held him off without much effort.

"Hello, Mr. Graham," Aunt Julia said with an added emphasis on the formality. "Thank you for the compliment as usual. How is Mildred?"

He waved off the name like a gnat flying around. "Just as vexing as ever. She's got this notion in her head that we're going to join that country club by Prospect Park. The Elm Square Men's Club, is it? Says she's been dying to take up tennis. The day I see my wife running after a tennis ball will be the day I keel over, it will." He clutched as his chest with his free hand, shaking his head.

Florence turned her head so as not to laugh right in the man's face. Apparently it didn't matter.

"And who is this?" His attention turned to her, revealing a yellowing smile split too wide.

"My niece, Miss Florence Winters. She's moved into the house with me. Florence, this is Flint Graham, one of Bryant Lumber's board members," Aunt Julia said with a polite smile that didn't quite reach her eyes. This man must have been someone she would rather not deal with.

"It's very nice to meet you, Mr. Graham," Florence said, wincing as he took her lace-gloved hand to kiss it. When he bent down she caught a whiff of stale cigars.

"The pleasure is all mine, my dear. My, you are a pretty young thing, aren't you? Sturdy like one of those willow trees in my backyard, too." He gave her a looking over. "You know, my son Filbert…"

"I hate to rush off like this, Mr. Graham, but we are needed in the ladies church group. I know you understand," Aunt

Julia swooped in before he had the chance to continue, clasping Florence's hand in hers. "I shall see you at the next quarterly meeting in December, I am sure."

Mr. Graham's face soured. "Of course. It was a pleasure to meet you, Miss Winters. Julia." He tipped his bowler hat at them and the two of them sped off through the crowd as Aunt Julia shook her head.

"That man. He's a thorn in the board's side. He never makes anything easy. Oh, how I wish Albert would've voted him out when he had the chance. It seems we're stuck with him now."

Florence hadn't expected her to go into detail about the family business in that way. It made her feel more like a confidante than just a niece. "How old is he?" she asked as they slid past a group of young children being escorted down a hall.

"I believe he is roughly twenty years my senior. Somewhere in his early seventies." Aunt Julia nodded and smiled at the woman bringing up the rear in the line of children.

"Someone ought to tell him about how retirement works," Florence said out of the corner of her mouth.

Aunt Julia glanced over at her and smiled. "Indeed."

The crowd of churchgoers spilled out of the building and into the front of the church's property where finally Florence caught sight of Mary-Ann Elmhurst hurrying along the sidewalk in a worn mink-lined fur coat. She didn't want to alert Aunt Julia—she could speak with her at another time—but Florence needed to talk to her on her own while she had the chance.

Luckily Aunt Julia had other things on her mind. "Do excuse me, Florence dear. I need to use the facilities."

Florence waited until she'd rounded the corner before quickly following after Mary-Ann, hoping she hadn't made a mistake in recognizing her.

At the corner of the block, cars and carts bustled past and Mary-Ann clutched at her coat, looking up and down the street.

"Hello, Mrs. Elmhurst," Florence said loudly over the noise of the city. "I just saw you in church and wanted to speak with you for a moment."

She realized at once that Mary-Ann had no idea who she was. Her eyebrows knitted together. "I'm sorry, I don't recall...?"

Florence cleared her throat and stuck out her hand, taking a moment to reintroduce herself. "Florence Winters. Sorry, I was introduced to you at the Montgomery Ward home appliance demonstration this past week."

Mary-Ann shook her hand, her eyes narrowing before it must have hit her. "Oh! Oh yes, I remember now. You're... Mrs. Bryant's niece?" There was no mistaking the frown that tugged at the corners of her small mouth.

She looked as though she couldn't have been much older than Florence, who wondered where her husband might be. Usually married couples would attend church services together, unless things were different here. But she glanced back over her shoulder and saw many of those instances.

"Yes," she finally said, giving her an encouraging smile. "And you and your cousin are friends with her." She ignored the look on Mary-Ann's face that said otherwise, already poised for the next part. "I heard about Mrs. Ramsey's disappearance. I am so very sorry. It must be very difficult for your family. Is there… is there anything that Aunt Julia or I might be able to help you with? I don't know a thing about the city, but I'm at your service if you need it."

She'd wanted to test Mary-Ann's reaction to bringing up Aunt Julia and oddly enough, Mary-Ann didn't look as concerned as she thought she might.

She only shook her head, her expression rather neutral for someone who probably thought Aunt Julia had a part to play in her cousin's sudden disappearance. "There isn't unless you know a good bet to beat Lucky Marty," she said with a sigh. But her eyes went wide quickly, her face contorting into quiet horror.

She'd said something she hadn't meant to.

Lucky Marty? Who in the world was he?

"I confess I have no connections with any jockeys or any of those *bets*," Florence tittered, trying to make light of the obvious slip. "Was Lucky Marty a friend of Mrs. Ramsey?"

Mary-Ann stared at her. No, Mary-Ann wasn't staring—she was studying her. She sucked in air between her teeth and motioned for the two of them to move over to the corner of the church's property. "My cousin, bless her, has enough side enterprises. She… Oh, I don't know why I'm even telling you. Perhaps because you don't know anything about anyone and I've been annoyed beyond my limits, who knows?"

Florence frowned. "I'm sorry, I don't follow."

With a dramatic roll of her eyes, Mary-Ann dropped her voice. "Adelaide has an affinity for things she shouldn't. And I hate to say it, but I'm not surprised if she's gotten into some kind of trouble."

Florence was stunned. For being her cousin, Mary-Ann sure did sound rather callous about it all. "But aren't you worried?" If it were one of her cousins, she most certainly would've been.

Mary-Ann withdrew a silver cigarette case from her pocket and held a matching silver lighter to a long cigarette, taking a careful drag of it as the tip burned orange. She blew the smoke away from Florence, then bit her lip. "I am worried about Adelaide, yes. But perhaps in different ways than most. I don't think she's hurt or worse, if that's what you mean."

"Florence!" someone called from behind them.

She turned to see Benny waving his hat to get her attention. He beamed at her, practically towering over the rest of the people milling around.

She waved back and when she turned, Mary-Ann was already walking away, the thin stream of smoke trailing behind her. It didn't take but a minute before she had fully disappeared into the mix.

Florence's shoulders slumped. Now what in the world was she supposed to make of any of *that?*

12

October 21, 1925

She scratched it out again, ready to toss the pen over her shoulder. After two days of keeping up with appearances for Aunt Julia's sake, she was desperate for some time to herself to think out loud about what Mary-Ann had told her Sunday morning.

She'd been introduced to Aunt Julia's friends as they'd come by to visit and discuss whether or not to carry on with the Ladies Christmas Luncheon planning while one of the heads of their group was still missing. And then she and Aunt Julia met with the mayor and his family to discuss some rather boring affairs dealing with the city needing more traffic towers at City Hall.

It wasn't that she didn't appreciate being brought along on these matters—really she did. It gave her much to look at and admire. The city was a treasure trove of excitement where around every corner you turned there was something new or interesting to see. And it was all so vast!

But these visits felt like they were at a most inopportune time. There were too many questions being added to the pile that grew each day, threatening to overflow onto the floor of her mind, and the last thing she needed to worry about was the number of street blocks in a part of the city that was conversationally called Hell's Kitchen.

With Ginny and her husband James visiting his family for the week, it left no one for Florence to discuss any of these questions with. She couldn't exactly go up to Hamish and ask for his opinion on whether Adelaide Ramsey was involved in any kind of unseemly business.

Though imagining the affronted look on his face was almost worth it.

She sighed, tapping the nib of the pen back into the ink well. It certainly didn't help that Aunt Julia hadn't taken Florence's and Mary-Ann's conversation seriously once she'd finally told her about it. She'd scoffed at what she called Mary-Ann's dramatics.

"I don't pretend to know what Adelaide gets up to, but this makes it sound like some sort of sordid affair. If Mary-Ann is so unbothered by her cousin's disappearance then she must know more than she's letting on. I'll have to bring that up with Detective Murray if he wishes to speak with me and Mr. Dredd again," she'd said over breakfast Monday morning before they'd headed out to meet with the heads of Gloriana House. There was a definite change in her spirits, though, once Florence had told her about Mary-Ann. She imagined it was a lightening of guilt and worry from her aunt's shoulders.

In fact, this morning Aunt Julia had decided she and Florence would go out for a pleasant breakfast at a nearby café where she proceeded to advise her on the many names in the town's highest social class. Now, if she would've been given faces to go with those many names, Florence might've had a better chance at remembering them.

She stared down at the little connections she'd written out on the paper and shook her head. It was just a bunch of scribbles really, nothing that felt like a complete thought at all.

Going back over everything yet again, she tried to focus on what little she did know. The first thing she'd really noticed was the name Mary-Ann had mentioned—Lucky Marty. Aunt Julia had waved off the name as nonsensical but Florence didn't think Mary-Ann would've said it just to be glib. It had to have been a slipup, she was sure.

She wrote out the name and equated it to the mysterious M. to whom Adelaide had been writing the letter. It could've been a coincidence, but she'd drawn a line connecting them all the same.

Lucky Marty = M.?

If Lucky Marty wasn't M., then who could he be? Was it even someone's real name? Or was Lucky Marty a name in disguise? Or a street name like Old Nick?

Florence groaned and wrote out Nicky Caboodles, adding a question mark. What if Lucky Marty was a place?

"But what was it she said about racing?" she wondered aloud, leaning back against her bed. "Is there perhaps a horse track around here somewhere?"

Could Lucky Marty be the name of a horse? Or even its jockey? She doodled a little horse in the corner of the page, unsure of where to go from here.

That's when she heard it... a soft scratching.

At first she thought she was imagining it. She was so wrapped up in unraveling this mystery that she was simply hearing things. Except she heard it even louder this time.

Her gaze darted toward the bedroom door as she put the fountain pen down. No. It wasn't coming from there.

There it was again, coming from the opposite side of the room instead. When she looked back over her shoulder she frowned. It sounded like it was coming from the closet...

What in the world?

She slowly rose from her perch on the bed to take careful steps over to the closet door, where the little scratches got even louder. The breath caught in her chest. She couldn't just write it off as a branch against the windowpane. This was certainly coming from the other side of the door.

Rationality was needed here, of course, but she crossed her fingers and silently hoped she wasn't about to meet her maker as she turned the knob and pushed in the door.

Something orange and fluffy dashed past her in a blur, scaring the pipes right out of her. Her voice screeched back into itself and she clutched at her chest. How many times would that darn cat try and give her a heart attack?

"You!" she ground out. "You have quite a knack for sneaking up on people, don't you? I suppose your name fits you to a T, *Sneaky*. Hmph." She shook her head at the fat orange cat that was now circling around the end of her bed.

"How in the world did you get yourself stuck in my closet anyhow? I would've known if you slipped past me... you're not that wily, you know."

Sneaky looked up at her with one lazy brown eye open before shutting it and tuning out Florence, who folded her arms.

"Well, I guess I'll just have to check then, won't I?"

A thorough sweep of the closet revealed that behind the assortment of shoes Florence hadn't looked through much was an opening to a vent of some sort, just barely wide enough for a person to fit into.

"Hmm. Must have come in through here and then couldn't find his way back out." She closed the closet door behind her, staring at the now snoozing cat.

"I suppose you can relax there if you'd like... I don't mind. Though something tells me you wouldn't care if I minded or not." And there she was again, talking to the pet as if he were a person who would answer her.

"Clearly I need to find someone else to talk to. Unless you have anything to add about Adelaide's disappearance?"

Sneaky opened his eyes until the narrow slits widened. He hadn't expected to be bombarded with questions.

"Ah, very good. Thanks for that." Florence sat down on the bed beside him to test the waters and see how he reacted to her presence. But Sneaky was a lazy cat if anything, and he most certainly did not care.

She ran her hand over his soft orange tufts of fur with an amused smile. "It's a shame you can't talk. I could use some help in trying to pin down this Lucky Marty guy. I don't know anyone who might be willing to help otherwise..." She trailed off. "Wait." Florence hopped up from the bed and went to look out the window.

Down below, the vivid blue body of Aunt Julia's car stuck out like a bluebird in a gray sky. Benny was wiping down the headlights with a rag before tucking it into his back pocket.

Benny! Maybe it was because he had to be more knowledgeable about the ins and outs of the city, but Florence thought perhaps he might have a better idea of who exactly Lucky Marty was.

She could only hope he'd be willing enough to tell her what he knew.

Pulling on a thinner black fringe cape instead of her usual wool coat, she slipped into a pair of black T-strap heels and hurried downstairs and out the back door that led to the carriage house.

The smell of motor oil was heavy in the air as she stepped out into the small building, looking around. There were two other vehicles here as well as the blue car parked outside past the brick arches—one was an older delivery truck, the other a sleek black Buick, which looked newly cleaned.

She followed the sound of the running engine, unable to help herself as she smiled. Benny was bent over, sifting through a large metal toolbox in one corner. Next to him stood a table with a shiny gramophone. A man was belting out a soulful tune in another language that Florence couldn't put her finger on. Spanish, maybe? Or something close to it... Italian, even?

Benny stood up, swaying a bit with the song, before twirling what she knew to be a socket wrench around in his fingers.

When he turned, his dark brown eyes went wide and deep ruby colored his high cheekbones.

"Oh, sorry, Miss Winters. I didn't see you there," he said loudly over the music.

She smiled again. "That's quite all right. I don't mean to interrupt you."

A thread of disappointment tugged in her as Benny went to stop the record. But he threw the rag over his shoulder and ran his hand through his thick, unruly hair. "No, no. I was just finishing up anyway." He tossed the socket wrench he'd just been searching for back into the open drawer as if to prove his point.

"Is there something I can help you with, somewhere you need to go?"

"Not exactly. Well, I did want to get your opinion on something if you don't mind," she said as he walked over.

"Of course. What is it, Miss Winters?"

"All right, let's start here. No more Miss Winters—it's Florence. I feel so odd and out of place being called that so formally all the time. If this is my home now, then I hope everyone can understand wanting to be called by my first name breathe in my own space." It all tumbled out at once, which was something she was not used to. Usually she picked her words carefully.

Benny folded his arms across his chest, the driver uniform tight across it. "Florence, huh?" A flash of a grin and he nodded. "And what did you need help with, *Florence?*"

She tried not to pay attention to the way he said her name in that sly manner and cleared her throat. "It's... it's actually somewhat complicated and, well, I have to know I can trust you." She found herself searching his face for any sign otherwise.

The amusement in his eyes changed a bit but he never let it slide away completely. "I'd like to think I'm trustworthy enough."

Really she didn't need to be too concerned with him keeping this to himself, but she hoped he would. "It's about Adelaide Ramsey's disappearance. I spoke with her cousin Mary-Ann at church on Sunday and I'm trying to figure out something she'd said to me."

He stood closer, his head tilted to one side. "Go on."

It was hard to be open, but she compelled herself to spill the truth about it all—how she'd embarrassingly sneaked her way into Adelaide's boudoir, to the conversations with Aunt Julia about her concerns.

When she was finished she was sure her cheeks were pink from the effort. It was a lot to rehash and Benny, to his credit, was an excellent listener.

He waited until he was sure she was done. "Huh. You sure have kept yourself pretty busy around here, haven't you?" His cracked smile broke the silence.

"Something like that," she said with the quirk of her mouth. "I'm just worried over this nonsense having to do with Aunt Julia. I don't want anything unseemly happening to her name with this kind of information floating about. I have a funny feeling that these types of things don't stay secret for very long."

He nodded. "Even in this big of a city, people talk."

"So Lucky Marty… I don't suppose you have any idea who he might be?" She very nearly crossed her fingers.

"I gotta admit, it sounds like the name of someone who would do business with Old Nick Colombo," he said, squinting his eyes. "But the name doesn't really ring any bells. Not that I'm all that familiar with those guys. But you hear things, you know. What do you think Mrs. Ramsey had to do with this guy?"

She blew away a strand of hair threatening to sweep across her brow. "I'm not sure. Maybe an affair? Or some kind of side business that Mary-Ann was alluding to? He could be anyone, really. Maybe even a code name for something else. That's the most puzzling part. That and the letter about Aunt Julia."

"Well I can tell you from experience that Adelaide Ramsey and your aunt don't see eye to eye, but yeah, it's strange she threw her on the tracks like that," Benny said, beckoning for her to follow him out to the blue car. He dropped down to wipe at something on the tires with the same rag. "Lucky Marty… yeah, I got nothing."

She sighed. At least she tried, anyway.

"I will say this—if this does have something to do with some kind of race, Old Nick handles the racing venues around here. I know one of his guys does a lot of business at Nicky Caboodle's setting up bets and whatnot. Groban, I think." He looked up at her and then past her toward the sky. "Don't know much about them past that, though."

Florence tilted her head to one side. "Is that a place you frequent?" It seemed funny to her, picturing Benny in a place called Nicky Caboodles.

Benny stood up and suddenly was a head taller than her, looking down at her a little closer than before. They both took a few steps back and Florence, without thinking, laughed nervously as the heat rose in her cheeks again.

"Frequent is a strong word," he said. "It isn't cheap, so I've only gone a few times. But the music's ace. I don't know if that helps anything but maybe it's worth checking into," he said, immediately turning around to wipe at the door handles of the passenger side of the car.

"That does help, actually." She blinked, not wanting to gawk at the poor man while he was just trying to get some work done. "And I think I know what to do now."

He threw her a look over his shoulder. "Glad to be of some assistance." That crooked grin hooked at the corner of his mouth again and she laughed.

"I do appreciate it. I wasn't sure if I should tell anyone about my trip to the Ramseys. You don't... you don't think I'm terrible for it, do you?" She was suddenly very invested in whatever his answer would be.

Still bent down, Benny turned to face toward her. "Not at all. You're worried about your aunt and I think that's pretty brave of you. Though I might be a little afraid of you now. Remind me never to cross you or I might go upstairs to find my apartment turned upside down." He gave her a wink.

She placed a hand on her hip and gave him a cheeky smile. "I'm glad we've come to an understanding."

Funny she hadn't realized Benny lived in the same place as her. She wondered what his apartment must look like past the concrete steps that led up to a small landing.

"Thank you again. I better get going if I'm going to figure this thing out." The October wind blew through the open air of the carriage house's courtyard, and Florence wrapped her cape around her even tighter.

He nodded when she went to turn. "Florence? Just be careful, all right? You don't want to get yourself all wrapped up in those guys' affairs. Believe me."

There was an edge to his words that she hadn't been expecting, and when she was on her way inside and heading into the reception room to make a call, she wondered how he must have known.

"Hello, I'd like to speak with Elizabeth Parnell, please," she told the operator, waiting until she heard the dial tone. A woman picked up and after a few more moments, Bitsy's pitched voice came over the line.

"Hello?"

Florence bit her lip. "Bitsy, it's Florence. Listen, I need your help..."

13

October 22, 1925

It had occurred to Florence that maybe there was a bit too much excitement in Bitsy's golden brown eyes when Florence had turned up on her front doorstep.

She had meant to choose her words wisely when she'd asked Bitsy if they could go check out Nicky Caboodle's together, but found that there was really no need. Bitsy was far too eager to oblige. Especially once she came to the conclusion that Florence was woefully unprepared for such a night.

"We'll have to find you some real nice glad rags to go out in obviously," she'd said as she looked Florence up and down with a skilled eye. "You'll clean up nicely in one of my Jeanne Lanvin numbers, I bet. Might have to have Griselda drop the waist a bit. You're awfully tall, aren't you?"

Florence rolled her shoulders back. "I wouldn't say *awfully* so, no. Five foot seven is a respectable height." Really, just because she wasn't the size of a pixie… "Oh, and I won't be needing any of your *glad rags*," she added, suddenly recalling the name Jeanne Lanvin. "I think I have a few of her dresses to choose from in my closet as well."

The fire in Bitsy's eyes died down same as the smile on her face. "Oh. All right. Maybe you'd like some help in choosing which one to flaunt?"

Florence hadn't meant to offend her and wanted to smack herself in the head for doing so. She was learning Bitsy lived life a bit unfiltered, and sometimes people like that didn't know when they came off rude. Honestly, Bitsy was a doll just for wanting to make friends with her.

Florence smiled warmly. "Obviously, I will need your professional advice. I'm not particularly used to going out to jazz clubs and I wouldn't want to look like a country bumpkin," she said smoothly.

That seemed to perk Bitsy right back up. "Swell! Then meet me here tomorrow at six o'clock sharp."

"That's pretty early on in the evening—I thought the doors don't open until nine?"

Bitsy waved her off. "Well, of course. But we'll need plenty of time to get ready and goodness knows I'll have to stand in for a lecture with my mother yet again."

Florence raised a brow. "A lecture? About going to Nicky Caboodle's?"

"Precisely. She isn't fond of the whole jazz scene, and hates when I go out with my cousins. You'd think she'd let me live my life; I mean, I am every bit of twenty as it is. But alas, we will most certainly be hearing a thing or two before we go out."

It seemed like nosy mothers were more universal than Florence had originally thought.

Bitsy danced around her, dabbing rouge along her cheeks, kohl around the lids of her eyes, curling her lashes, and pausing to ever so carefully line Florence's lips in a muted red that Florence was nervous about. She'd never been one for wearing much makeup, but she'd hardly ever had the chance to make it count.

A jazz club was certainly not her cup of tea, or at least she didn't think it would be. But then again, she hadn't had the chance to test that theory just yet.

"Flo, you look fabulous!" Bitsy squealed as she stood back to admire her handiwork. "A Brooksy! A real knock-em-dead! Look at those lashes, gal; I didn't know you had it in you!"

"Florence," she corrected, but blushed anyway as she spun around on Bitsy's vanity chair to take a look in the mirror.

She had to admit, Bitsy knew her stuff.

The rouge on her cheeks highlighted her cheekbones, and the mascara and kohl highlighted her long, feathery lashes and deep green eyes. Somehow Bitsy had made her lips into the perfect cupid's bow, and her face didn't look like it was covered in flour. Her makeup was not loud, but not understated. It was exactly where Florence had wanted it—lovely.

"Oh my, Bitsy. You've outdone yourself," she said softly, patting at her face in disbelief. "Thank you."

"Yeah, yeah, don't go all soft on me." Bitsy shrugged her thin shoulder gracefully, looking mollified. "And you had doubts?"

"Me? Never." Florence stood up and walked over to the large floor-length mirror that took up a good portion of Bitsy's boudoir, Bitsy joining her.

They looked quite the pair standing together, and they smiled widely at one another.

"We'll be turning heads left and right, Flo. Just you watch!" Bitsy said, swishing her gold dropped-waist fringe dress with a laugh. She was done in a white-and-gold-embroidered headband to cover her blonde hair, and wore gold and mauve eyeshadow to match her dress and lips. The dress hung down on her petite body perfectly, and Florence thought it was rather funny to see their height difference even in their heels. Bitsy was easily half a foot shorter.

But Florence couldn't help but stare at her own reflection. After much deliberation, she and Bitsy had settled on a sleeveless sea-green satin evening dress that hung from her shoulders down to the drop-waist, gathering a bit there before hitting her knees. The border down the middle was a muted peacock-inspired strip edged in black beading, which happened to match everything else they'd picked to go with the outfit: emerald drop earrings in sterling, a black-and-silver-beaded handbag, and shiny silver heels with thin straps and sea-green beading.

It was outside of her usual comfort, but Florence stood up straight and tilted her head to the side, imagining if this was what Louise Brooks and Aileen Pringle felt like whenever they were in costume.

"I think it's about time, don't you? I'm sure Harold already has the Buick running, so we'd better go," Bitsy said, handing Florence the luxurious fur-lined, silk-embroidered coat that she had draped over her arm. "And a finishing touch here. Don't look at me like that; you're not wearing that wool coat of yours with this dress. It's simply too stunning to cover up."

Florence was more worried about the actual October weather than how her coat looked, but she sighed and took the coat. "If you insist."

Much to Bitsy's surprise and relief, her parents were nowhere to be found when she and Florence were heading out the door. "Phew! We might actually be a little early in that case. Shame, that. I like showing up fashionably late."

Harold, her driver, made quick work of driving across the Brooklyn Bridge to Prospect Park as Bitsy had noted, pointing out places of interest to her as they went. Luckily the car had an enclosed cabin and they didn't have to worry about the evening wind.

You could see and hear the jazz club from a block back, not only from the lively music piping through the entrance but because of the line of people waiting to get in. Florence frowned, imagining standing out in the line with such a thin dress on. Her hosiery was not going to withstand the cold, that was for sure.

"Thanks, Harold," Bitsy said with a wink as the two of them pulled up to the front of Nicky Caboodle's.

Florence stared up at the place, her eyes wide. It must have been pretty impressive during the daytime but nothing would compare to how the dazzling lights illuminated their way inside. They blinked all around the marquee where the name Nicky Caboodle's was lit up in electric blue seemed to dance along with red music notes all around it. Besides the long line of people waiting to get in, there were cars all along the road, waiting to let people out at the front door.

Just like Harold had done with them.

"Don't we have to wait down there?" Florence asked, glancing toward the end of the line.

Bitsy scoffed. "Hardly! My father rubs shoulders with some people inside, so I'm let in right here." She linked Florence's arm in hers. "Come on, Flo. It's time to show you off."

"But I—" She was whisked away before she had a chance to finish.

Without much fanfare, Bitsy waggled her fingers at one of the bouncers outside of the club who moved out of the way for the pair of them to pass. Florence still couldn't believe her luck. Part of her felt bad for those people standing out in the cold, but that quickly dissipated when she found herself standing inside the place.

The lights that had been blazing bright outside the jazz club were dim and more subdued inside, adding a layer of intrigue to the red velvet draped along the walls, casting shadows on those already inside. Even the chandeliers gave off a low, warm light.

And oh, the people! Dressed to the nines, men and women both. Men in their fedoras and perfectly tailored suits, some of them reminding her of Douglas Fairbanks, women in lavish gowns with sultry smiles. A strange mix of perfume and cigar smoke laced the warm air.

Florence was glad to be rid of the heavy coat when the coatroom attendant took theirs. Bitsy steered them toward a table in the middle, gesturing for her to take a seat.

She sat down in the red-velvet-backed seat, her eyes wide as Bitsy giggled next to her.

"Isn't this the bee's knees? And look, I told you people would stare!" She casually looked over her shoulder at a couple of men who were eyeing her and Florence with interest. "How could they not?"

Florence wasn't sure how to feel about that. "I don't suppose with you being a regular around here that you know any of the people who work here, do you?" She'd nearly forgotten her whole reason for coming here in the first place. It wasn't as if she'd really divulged this to Bitsy, either.

"Oh, sure!" she said a little loudly. "I know a few of the musicians and some of the entertainers. A couple of them are friends. I don't know many people by name, only their faces. It's kinda hard to have a whole conversation with them in a place like this, you know."

Florence nodded. "So I've heard. But I've also heard that some people conduct their business here too, so it couldn't be too hard."

Waiters were circling the place, taking orders and bringing out drinks as more and more people sat down. It took Florence until now to realize the tables were placed strategically around a large dance floor polished and shining under the lights above.

"Probably," Bitsy said as she adjusted her headband. She leaned in closer. "I've heard some of the bosses like to do that. It makes sense since this is Old Nick's place."

"Benny—sorry—our driver told me that Old Nick has a guy who handles booking the bets on races in here. Have you heard about that?" Florence asked.

"I know of him, yeah. I don't know his name, but I think I've seen him around. He's kinda tall, stays in a pin-striped suit and white fedora, looks sort of like Buster Keaton. Why?" Bitsy grinned. "You looking to gamble or something?"

Florence quickly shook her head. "Not at all, I was just curious. I figure it's good for one to know her surroundings. This place really is lovely, Bitsy. Thanks for coming with me." She didn't want to seem overly eager to talk about this Groban guy, but it was good to know he might be around here this evening.

The waiter, impeccably dressed in an all-white suit, came by to take their orders. Just the mention of chicken paella made Florence's stomach growl. Luckily no one could hear it over the din of the room.

The stage was lit up in spotlights all pointing to the matching red velvet curtain hiding away the rest of it. There was a microphone stand placed right in the middle.

A man in a powder-blue suit and black bow tie walked onto the stage, smiling and waving at the patrons on the floor. Everyone stopped to pay attention and clap, some people letting out whistles of approval.

Bitsy squealed and squeezed Florence's hand with a grin.

"Ladies and gentlemen! I welcome you to our humble establishment," the man said into the microphone before giving a slight bow. "Here at Nicky Caboodle's, we delight in providing our guests with the time of their lives, which is exactly what we plan to do tonight. I'm your host for the evening, Maxwell Devonshire, but since we're all friends now, you can call me Mad Max!"

Florence followed everyone else's lead and clapped enthusiastically.

Mad Max did a little tap dance behind the microphone and laughed, waving everyone off. "You folks don't want none of that—after all, you're here to be entertained! What's on the menu tonight, folks?"

On his cue, the curtains slowly pulled back to reveal a large jazz band wearing matching blue suits and jovial smiles. There was more clapping and even more whistles.

"Oh, these guys behind me? You've heard of them, have you? Let me introduce you fine folks to the Kid Oliver Players!"

The band broke out in an upbeat tune in response, the players swaying from the left to the right in perfect synchronization until the drummer hit his snare.

Mad Max went on to introduce the entertainment for the night, featuring a trio of women singing along with the band, as well as a dance number being put on by none other than the Ziegfeld Follies girls.

Florence's jaw dropped. "As in *the* Ziegfeld Follies? On the radio?"

Bitsy giggled, shimmying when the band took off with their first song of the night. "Absolutely! My friend Delia, you'll see her since she's one of the singers in the Cherry Trio, she's been dying to try out for them. I don't think she'll have any problem at all; I mean she's already a regular on the *Twilight Hour* radio show. Have you heard that one yet? I'll have to introduce you to her and Matthew! You'll just adore them, I know it."

It wasn't long before dinner was served, but Florence was surprised at just how much she was enjoying the entertainment part of the night. The band was loud and lively, with the lead, a man named Clarence, dancing around everyone with his saxophone. It was hard not to tap your toes in time with it all.

"Mmm, this is delicious," she said a little too enthusiastically as she bit into the chicken. She made a mental note to swing by the kitchen and ask Chef Auguste if he would try it out at home.

Bitsy bobbed along to the music, nodding. "And how. You can't go wrong with their dinner plates here. One of the best on this side of the East River."

She nearly hopped out of her seat when the three women Mad Max introduced as the Cherry Trio sauntered up onstage. "There's my gal! Delia's the one in the middle. Isn't she a beauty?"

Florence was stunned—Bitsy was absolutely right. Delia's deep auburn hair was finger-combed and shined under the lights; her low-cut black chiffon dress swung with its beading, matching the other two women on either side of her. She was the epitome of gorgeous and elegant, from her stylish makeup and long, black satin gloves to the way her sultry voice crooned into the microphone. Florence could see why Bitsy would become friends with her.

The next song by the Cherry Trio was a fast one, and nearly everyone went out onto the floor to dance along.

Bitsy yanked at Florence's hand. "Come on, Flo, let's get out there and sweep!"

"Ha, that's funny, Bitsy. I think I'll just sit tight and enjoy the music from here. Oh look, one of those dashing young men over there is making goo-goo eyes at you!" She nodded her chin to the pair of men who had been checking them out earlier.

"No, ma'am, you're not going to sit here all sad and lonely—"

"I promise you, I won't be lonely. I'll be quite content, in fact," Florence interrupted.

Bitsy put her hand on her hip. "No fair, Flo. You can't come out to a jazz club and not dance. Why, that's half the fun!" She pulled at Florence's hand harder. She had some strength for a little thing like her.

"Ladies? May I... be of some assistance?"

They both turned to see an angelic-looking young man with curls the color of gold and a dark, high-waisted suit and tie standing there, brow raised and smile wide.

Florence bit her lip. "I'm sorry, we're actually—"

"Matthew, darling! There you are! I was wondering where you'd gone to," Bitsy cried out, throwing her arms around Matthew's neck.

Florence blinked. Well, that was not what she was expecting.

Matthew waggled his eyebrows at Bitsy and tipped a dark glass back before looking over at Florence. "And who's this lovely woman? A new friend of yours, Bits?"

"Indeed she is; this is my friend Miss Florence Winters. She's Julia Bryant's niece, and she's living in with the dame."

Matthew stuck out his hand with an arched brow. "Florence. Nice to meet you, darling. I'm Matthew Sheffield. Resident piano player."

She took his hand and smiled. "Nice to meet you."

Bitsy snorted. "That's not the only kind of player..."

"You wound me, Bits!" Matthew said, pretending to clutch at his heart. "I think I shall never recover."

"You're such a drama queen, Matty. When are you going onstage tonight, anyway?" she asked with an eye roll.

Matthew folded his arms across his chest with an air of indifference. "It's not my night, thankfully. I'm just here for Delia. Moral support and all of that."

That made sense to Florence. Delia and Matthew would make a very handsome couple. "Oh, are you two a couple?" she asked, immediately regretting it when he and Bitsy burst into raucous laughter.

"That's a good one, Florence, I commend you. Delia is my cousin, actually. Not to mention she's... not at all my type." He flashed her an enigmatic smile. "I did come over to ask why you ladies aren't out on the floor."

Bitsy jutted her thumb toward Florence. "This one doesn't like to dance."

Florence put her hand on her hip. "Hmph. I never said that. I just... well, I'm just not a fan of dancing in front of other people is all."

Matthew and Bitsy shared a knowing look that frankly made her nervous.

"I think it's time to remedy that, my lady," Matthew said, sweeping her up onto her feet. "Let's blouse."

She was pulled out onto the dance floor with a shimmying Bitsy right behind her.

There was simply no way out of it, not with Matthew leading her. He smiled down at her with a sort of sly look about him. "Don't be so nervous. Just follow my lead. Do you know the shimmy?"

"Er..." Her eyes darted around the room, wishing she had a way to suddenly know how to answer that.

"Okay then, just follow my lead. It's pretty simple." He shook his shoulders, took a step forward and a step back before holding his hand out for hers. "See? Your turn."

Florence swallowed hard but took his hand and tried it out on her own. Well, she wasn't stepping on anyone's toes anyhow.

"There you go! Now throw your hips into it a little, like this."

"Go, Flo, go!" Bitsy called out, shimmying along with him.

Florence laughed, covering her mouth as she gave it a go, trying to keep up with the pair of them. The music seemed to circle around them as the lead man yelled out to the band.

"Get hot! Get hot!" the players in the band yelled, encouraging everyone to dance and twirl even more. Women grabbed the hems of their dresses, doing the Charleston with their beaus who had left their hats on the tables, everyone sweating in the throng of people.

Bitsy took her hand this time and spun her around even more, and everything was a blur. Florence laughed despite herself.

The moment the song was over, Matthew bowed and kissed her hand. "Thank you for the dance, my lady. I'm afraid I have a prior engagement, but I'm sure I'll see you around."

She pushed her hair back past her ear. "Thanks, Matthew. It was nice meeting you."

He pretended to tip his hat before disappearing into the thick of the dance floor. Bitsy was pulling Florence back to their table, fanning at herself with her hand.

"Boy, that was fun! And you said you couldn't dance." She gulped down nearly half of her water.

"I said no such thing," Florence said, watching as a familiar face approached them from the side of the room with the dry bar.

Bitsy followed her gaze and waved as Delia came over to take a seat across from them. "We heard you up there showing off your pipes. Was that a new one?"

Delia pulled out a cigarette holder and a thin cigarette to place in it. "Just a little ditty Greta came up with last week. Did you like it? I wasn't sure it had enough oomph, but it seems like people liked it well enough. Thanks for the smoke in advance," she said, leaning over for Bitsy, who had pulled out a lighter to light her thin cigarette.

The smoke streamed out in a circle as she looked over at Florence, her kohl-outlined eyes warm. "Hello, darling. Who might you be?"

"Florence Winters. I'm a friend of Bitsy's. And you must be Delia Harris. She was just telling me about you. You have a beautiful voice, and I really did like the song."

Delia's eyes sparkled in appreciation. "You're a peach. Well," she said, sticking her other gloved hand out, "it's a pleasure to meet you. Any friend of Bitsy's is a friend of mine. I take it you've met my cousin?"

Florence nodded with a laugh. "I did, indeed. He's a swell dancer. I was hard at work to keep up with him."

"I'm willing to bet. Where'd he run off to?"

Bitsy sighed. "You know where."

Delia crossed her arm underneath the other, taking a long drag from her cigarette. "How unfortunate. I told him about staying away... he's going to wind up heartbroken yet again."

Florence frowned. Matthew seemed too kind a person to deserve his heart broken.

"You can't tell him nothing. We've talked about it at great lengths, and every time he tells me he's done but then he's right back at it. I wish Edward would just leave him alone," Delia said with a scowl twisting her pretty features.

Florence blushed hard and looked away. She had certainly not been expecting that, and she wasn't quite sure of what to say, so she nodded along. Matthew was a darling, and who was she to judge anyone, really? Anyone who could make her move in a way that didn't have her looking like a stiff scarecrow was a-okay in her book.

If there was one thing she was learning during her time in New York City, it was that there was a big wide world out there that was beyond her experience.

Florence's stomach knotted. She'd completely forgotten about Groban! Good gracious, she was in such a tizzy with the dancing that she could've easily gone home before remembering.

"Delia, I hate to interrupt but do you know anything about Old Nick's bookie who does his racing business here? I… was just curious about the races. My, er, friend loves to go to the races and I'd like to find out more about them in case she comes for a visit as a surprise." It was a very stretched truth—Bernice had gone to a few horse races with her fiancé, though Florence would hardly call her a fan. And perhaps if she did visit they might do the same, but she doubted it.

"Races? That would be Bill Groban. He runs the races at Belmont Park and Landing Downs as well as… well, it's not exactly legal, but he handles the races at Elm Square. Greyhounds. They shut the whole thing down in New York earlier this year but someone might have opened up a new underground ring there months back," Delia said, flicking ash into the ashtray. "But you certainly didn't hear that from me. Is your friend into greyhound racing?"

Florence quickly nodded. "Oh, yes. It's at Elm Square, you said? Is that the men's club you were telling me about, Bitsy?"

"The one and only, but wow! I had no idea they were running dog races there! Man, I'm really out of the loop." She pouted.

Florence needed to nudge the conversation back. "Is he here tonight, by any chance? Bill Groban?"

Delia shook her head and Florence sighed. "He's usually at the races on Thursdays and Fridays, though. So you can catch him there tomorrow night if the two of you go."

A light bulb went off in her head. Bitsy had already told her that her father was a member at the men's club. Perhaps she could get her in there like she was able to get her into Nicky Caboodle's?

Bitsy seemed to be thinking the same thing. "Hmm. Well, I'm not much for races—I think betting's a bore, to be honest—but I'd be happy to take you out there sometime if you'd like, Flo."

Florence couldn't help but smile. It was nearly a shot in the dark, and who was to say that Lucky Marty had anything to do with the place? But it was a start, at least. If anything, maybe she'd overhear someone either talking about Lucky Marty being there or perhaps mention the name in regards to one of the other racing venues Old Nick apparently operated.

"That sounds swell, Bitsy. I might just take you up on the offer."

14

October 23, 1925

Despite the gloomy cloud cover hovering over the neighborhood, the morning light pierced through one of Florence's bedroom windows, provoking her to chuck a satin pillow in its general direction.

She groaned. It had been a late night out with Bitsy the night before, and even though she kept to her fizzy drinks and water at Nicky Caboodle's, she was still nursing a headache. Cracking one eye open, she tried to focus on the blurry clock on the wall until she could make out the time.

Nine thirty. She groaned again.

It took some doing, but once she'd hopped into the shower and towel-dried her hair, she was quick to get dressed for the day and make her way downstairs for breakfast.

Aunt Julia eyed her with interest as she entered the breakfast room. "Good morning, Florence."

Florence fought back a yawn and smiled. "Good morning. I apologize for being late. I didn't have the best sleep, it seems." She noticed Aunt Julia had already set her silverware across her plate, finished with her meal.

"It's quite all right, dear. Are you not feeling well?"

"Oh, I'm fine now. And hungry, no less. What's on the menu this morning?" Maybe some food and coffee might help with the headache.

"I asked for a light breakfast myself. Vienna rolls, some fresh fruit, and a cup of Earl Grey. I'm sure the chef can make whatever you'd like. He's in quite a good mood from what I can tell." She folded her napkin neatly and placed it on top of the empty plate and silverware.

Something soft and silky brushed past Florence's legs, giving her a fright before she realized the orange bundle of fluff responsible was bounding toward Aunt Julia as she rose from her seat.

"Off with you," she said with a stern voice, fixing Sneaky with a knowing look. "You know you're not allowed in the eating rooms."

"Or the kitchen for that matter," Ginny said with a smirk, winding around the table with a crate of fresh flowers. "Good morning Missus, Miss," she said with a little curtsy.

"Good morning!" Florence beamed at her. She decided if it made Ginny more comfortable not to informally address her in front of Aunt Julia then she'd respect it. Why put her friend in discomfort over a silly little thing?

The cat let out a fitful sneeze, bringing the attention back to him.

"Don't make me drag you out myself, Sneaky," Ginny warned him, nudging him with her foot. "Move it."

Sneaky stared up at her in silence for a moment. He arched his back with a lazy yowl before parking his rear end on the floor at her feet, his fluffy tail swishing from side to side.

Florence couldn't help it—she giggled.

"Sneaky, boy! Out with you!" Aunt Julia said, smacking her hand down on the table. He shot out of the room like a bullet, all three women shaking their heads after him. Ginny winked at Florence before following in the same direction.

Florence's stomach growled, not so gently reminding her that she was here for a reason. "You know, some fresh fruit does sound—"

The doorbell rang throughout the first level of the house, cutting Florence off. Hamish seemed to materialize out of nowhere, rushing into the grand room to answer it.

A few moments later he returned, his face ashen. "Mrs. Bryant, Detective Marshall is here requesting to speak with you. He says it is urgent."

Florence gasped, looking between the pair of them. *Oh no.*

Pulling herself up to her full height, Aunt Julia gave Hamish a curt nod and left the room, with him following right after.

All Florence could do was sit, her stomach clenched tightly and no longer interested in food. In fact, when Chef Auguste came out to greet her with a bowl of fresh fruit, she thanked him but could barely pick at it. Forcing some strawberries and grapes down the hatch, she folded her napkin and drummed her fingers along the tabletop.

She was just about to go investigate the matter when Aunt Julia returned to the breakfast room, her face pale and drawn.

With her hands clasped tightly in front of her, she sighed. "The news is not good, I'm afraid. Detective Marshall just informed me that one of the Ramsey automobiles was found pushed into the East River late last night."

Florence clapped her hand to her mouth. "No," she said softly. "Please tell me… they didn't find her in it, did they?"

"He didn't mention if they'd retrieved a body, no. I asked if she'd been found and he said no. But one can only assume that the vehicle was there on purpose."

"That's what the police think? What does Mr. Ramsey say? Do they know which vehicle?" Hadn't she overheard Adelaide mentioning how she liked to drive herself?

If she was surprised her niece was asking so many questions, Aunt Julia did not let on. "They found the vehicle when one of the pier crews down Pike Slip—which is a major dock area for ships and boats on the East River—noticed the bubbles from the water early this morning. There were marks on the road leading up to the docking area. The police have only just managed to hoist the vehicle out of the water, and according to Edward Ramsey, it was not his vehicle but Adelaide's. Apparently she had her own vehicle that she would drive around, and it was not mentioned to me before, but it had been missing as well."

Florence wrung her hands together. The car had been missing too? And now it was found in the East River? None of this sounded promising. Her heart lurched as she thought of how Mr. Ramsey and Mary-Ann must have felt.

Surely Mary-Ann would be more concerned now, with the update.

A thought occurred to her and she waited a moment, not wanting to blurt it all out without thinking on it. "Edward Ramsey... have the police checked into his whereabouts during the time they think the car may have crashed into the river?"

Aunt Julia nodded, clearing her throat as if to rid it of something unpleasant. "Detective Marshall explained that Edward was tied up in business affairs at the time."

At this, Florence raised a brow. "Business affairs?" She didn't want to say much because it also occurred to her that Aunt Julia herself seemed to conduct business affairs late at night.

"That is what he claims, yes. And the detective has reason enough to accept his statement on it, so I will not challenge it."

It was hard not to want to poke at the validity of his statement a little, but Florence could tell Aunt Julia thought the matter was not up for debate. "I see. Were you able to also have your name cleared from having anything to do with this terrible news?"

Aunt Julia's gaze slid to the floor. "Not as I had hoped, I'm afraid. He took Hamish's and Virginia's statements on my whereabouts last night, and before you say anything, no, you will *not* be giving your own," she said, effectively cutting off Florence as she opened her mouth in protest. Aunt Julia whipped her gaze toward her. "I'll not have you getting involved in the matter. Is that understood?" There was a harsh finality to her words, leaving a bitter taste in Florence's mouth. She wasn't a fan of being shut down so swiftly.

She bit back the reply she was ready to give out, drawing in a slow steadying breath before saying, "Yes, ma'am."

Aunt Julia studied her face intently before she nodded and left the room.

Maybe she wouldn't *directly* involve herself with the police department, but Florence simply wasn't in the mood to debate semantics. She'd do what she thought was necessary and that was that.

It wasn't long before Florence had slipped her fingers into her leather gloves and her arms into her crimson wool coat, tying a scarf around her neck on this blustery day as she journeyed down the street toward Bitsy's again.

❀

WITH SOME HELP FROM BITSY, Florence was once again dressed to play the part—this time the part of a wealthy single woman looking for an even wealthier husband. It most certainly wasn't her idea of a fun costume, but Bitsy insisted it was necessary.

"Say what you will, Flo, but even I have to be careful with the way I go about visiting Elm Square. It is a men's club after all. They don't let just any old floozy inside. You have to act like your presence will add to the overall look of the place. Like a pretty vase of flowers."

Florence groaned, slipping on a pair of Bitsy's kidskin gloves up her forearm. "How I just love depending on the male courtesy to be allowed into places," she said, the sarcasm cutting deeper than she meant.

Bitsy sighed and adjusted the heavy fur coat she'd insisted Florence wear. "None of that, now. If you spout off with that at the door, you'll be dumped out front on your tuchus. Believe me, they're particular. It's best to play it safe if you want in. Speaking of... do you really think your friend would want to go through all of this just to do some gambling? I promise the horse races at Belmont Downs are an easier bet. Quite literally, in fact." There was a sort of pride in her eyes at her own pun.

Despite the new insightfulness Bitsy was showing, Florence still hadn't told her the real reason behind their outings. She wasn't sure if she ever would, but she supposed that all depended on the end results. "Bernice loves dogs. I'm sure she'd appreciate me going through the effort."

A frown pulled down at the corner of Bitsy's mouth. "Maybe, but I don't think they treat the dogs particularly well. Or at least that's what I heard." She shrugged. "But if you say so."

Something pitted in Florence's belly. She hated the thought of those sweet dogs being taken advantage of, if that was the case. Perhaps there was a way to... but she shook her head free of the extra thoughts. First she needed to find out about this Lucky Marty, if she could.

Hopefully her luck would play out well today.

"I believe this is the part where someone yells 'showtime!'" Florence said, stepping out of the Parnell family Buick and up to the Elm Square Men's Club. She stared at the front doors and shoved her hands deep into her pockets.

Bitsy smiled but said nothing, tugging at Florence's arm to follow her.

Boy, she wasn't lying when she said they had to be careful going in. Even though he knew her father, the gentleman behind the lobby check-in was dubious over their arrival.

"We don't generally let women in without their male counterpart," he said dryly, folding his wiry arms across his chest. "And I don't see where your father is here."

Bitsy drew her coat tighter around herself and leaned in. "My father helped pay to build this place, good sir. If you'd like, we can certainly ring him up to see how he would feel about his dearest child being denied a simple game of tennis with her friend. What did you say your name was again?" It all came off with a cool air of confidence that Florence hadn't expected from her. The more time she spent with Bitsy, the more she learned that there was more to her than meets the eye.

The man narrowed his eyes at her. "I didn't. Though... I suppose we can let it slide this once. Next time, you will need to have him present to be let in, however. In case it slips your mind again." He pulled out a clipboard and ran his finger down the length of paper, jotted something down, and gestured for the two of them to move on before muttering awfully loudly, "Some getup for a game of tennis."

Bitsy rolled her eyes as they headed deeper into the club. "Now to find out where this racetrack is... I can't imagine it being out on the grounds. Much harder to hide it that way, though Old Nick tends to get away with a lot more than he should." She tucked her gloves into her pocket. "Everyone who's anyone knows it."

Looking down one wide marble-floored hallway she said quietly, "Let's try looking around inside first. I know where almost everything is, so it could only be in a few other places I've never taken the time to really look at."

"You're the captain of this ship," Florence said just as quietly, imploring her to take the lead.

It took some doing, but after several missteps down corridors that led to cigar and brandy rooms thick with smoke, a billiards room, and a fancy indoor pool with lap lanes and people splashing about in the water, Florence and Bitsy managed to find an offshoot from the pool room that led to a long hallway with only two doors along it. The first door led to a janitor's closet, but the second, which was oddly named Private Personnel Only, led elsewhere.

It was rather dark in the twisting stairwell that seemed to go down forever, and several times Bitsy looked back over her shoulder and up at Florence, a flash of apprehension in her eyes.

But they continued on until they reached their destination. The very place they'd been hoping for—the greyhound racing venue.

The room was large, large enough to fit what looked like a dirt-packed running track with several stands for people to watch from around it. In fact, she wouldn't have even called it a room per se, but more of a hangar or warehouse of sorts. Florence felt like she'd walked into a whole new world.

There were bright lights set high above the room, turning the underground area into a space that mimicked being lit up by the sunshine outside. The area was louder than any of the other places they'd checked, with the sound echoing in the large space, full of both people and dogs.

There weren't any races going on, but there were still plenty of people milling about. Some were dressed just the same as her and Bitsy, flaunting their wealth and status with ease. Some wore working trousers and suspenders covered in dirt, while others were wearing sportier clothes that made sense for other parts of the club.

"If you were the guy running the scene, where would you be?" Florence said out loud, more rhetorically than anything.

"No clue. But we could try looking closer to where they keep the dogs."

Florence arched a brow at her. "What makes you think Groban would be there?"

Bitsy just shrugged and gave her an angelic smile. "No particular reason. I just want to see the pooches." And off she went, strutting as if she belonged here with the rest of them.

"I suppose it wouldn't hurt anyway," Florence said to herself, quick to catch up with Bitsy.

They passed the cage pits at the beginning of the track where numbers one through eight were painted in different colors on top of the enclosures, marking each dog's lane. When they got closer to where the kennels were, Florence found a few trailers and even a smaller building nearby, with a few men talking among themselves. None of them seemed to notice their presence.

"Oh! Well, would you look at that!" Bitsy cried, pointing to the kennels. "Pooches! Let's go take a look at the dears. Then you can ask around for the bets."

Florence swallowed, more desperate to listen in to the men's conversation than looking at the dogs. "I... I'll be right there. Let me just go..."

Luckily Bitsy had already taken off toward the kennels, leaving Florence to gradually get closer to the group of men, pretending to study one of the smaller signs hung up outside the small building with the race times written on it in white chalk.

They appeared to be deep in conversation. One of the men, a head shorter than the other two and dressed in work trousers, rubbed at the back of his neck. "I don't know, Freddy. The pit's gotta get cleaned out by Saturday night, you know that. Neither of us got time to handle Bill's slips."

The man in the newsboy cap took a long drag off a cigarette before dropping it and scuffing it into the ground with his boot. "How long is it gonna take to clean out a bloomin' pit, mate? If Bill says we handle the slips, then we handle the bloody slips. I'm not giving the chap a reason to side-eye me, and you'd be slick to do the same."

The taller of the three men sighed and Florence tried to lean her head closer to hear him.

"Groban won't care who does what, as long as it gets done. Freddy, you can handle the slips and Lyle and I will prep the pits," the more soft-spoken man replied with a shrug. "This time, make sure the lanes have been dragged. After what happened last time with the rocks in Great Scot's pit... I don't wanna have to see no more of them poor guys having to get doctored up. It ain't right. And we'll have to help Sunday morning, keeping an eye out. You know people get shady on the double winnings games."

None of what they were saying helped Florence much other than the mention of Bill Groban. But it didn't look like he was anywhere nearby, and with a frown, she walked over and leaned against the side of the smaller building.

What she needed to do was to find a... she looked down at the sleeve of Bitsy's luxurious fur coat and gasped. "Of course you would, you fool," she mumbled to herself, licking at her fingers to try and wipe the white chalk off of the edge of the very expensive coat. "Bitsy is going to murder me."

She whipped around to see where it had come from and was face-to-face with a large chalkboard taller than her with the numbers one through eight written out, each number representing a different dog.

Number one... Here Today Gone Tomorrow. Number two... Peachy Keen. Number three... Heaven's Angel. Florence followed the names all the way down the board until...

Number seven was Lucky Marty! Florence nearly squealed with surprise as she read the name scribbled on the chalkboard in wide letters. The bets were heavily in the dog's favor, it seemed, higher than any of the other seven dogs. If she had to guess, Lucky Marty was the champion of the bunch.

A raucous eruption of barking dogs tore her attention away as the eight greyhounds were let out into the main kennel together, all of them jogging around and happy for the space from wherever they'd come.

Bitsy was hanging around outside the kennel and Florence could already hear her crooning at the nearest dogs, waving to them as if they were children.

She smiled. They were some beautiful creatures: elegant, smart from the looks of it, and generally content. They must have recently been fed.

She wondered which dog was which and glanced at the sign, imagining which name matched each dog best. If she had to guess, the charcoal gray one with the shiny green-and-gold collar was Lucky Marty. He looked like he would be the fastest out of them, not to mention the colors of the collar.

What was it that Mary-Ann had mentioned about him? She had said something about winning against him. Perhaps he was the one to beat and Adelaide was a gambling sort of woman.

Maybe it wouldn't be such a bad idea to look more into Bill Groban. If Adelaide had a sort of shoddy record with them here, perhaps she was in deeper than just some losing bets. The thought twisted in the middle of her chest. Old Nick didn't sound like he was the most accommodating fellow, either.

Florence couldn't see which dog the spotted fawn-and-white dog was—the tags that hung from his thin neck were too far to read from where she was standing—but she smiled at it, silently wishing it the best. It was trotting around quietly, looking like a sweetheart if ever she saw one. She wasn't the only one to admire the dog, as one of the men in the kennels patted the dog's head before opening up another gate to let a woman inside.

Did Bitsy know they were allowed to go pet the dogs? She didn't think that made much sense personally, especially in an open space with several competitive dogs over half her height. But the woman didn't seem to mind, being only slightly taller than Bitsy herself.

The woman waved at the man and reached over to scratch the dog under his thin muzzle, leaning down to talk to him. The dog shook out his head, his long tongue lolling out of his mouth as she rubbed his back.

When the man let her back outside of the kennel and shut the door behind them, the woman turned around. It was hard to make out her face with the bright lights above casting long shadows against the large straw hat that was covering so much of her head. She tightened the belt around her tweed wrap-over coat, adjusted the thick yellow wool scarf around her neck, and slipped past Bitsy to disappear behind one of the trailers. Even out of Florence's line of sight she could hear the woman's sneezing fit.

Dogs were sweet enough animals, but she couldn't help but wonder why anyone would visit a bunch of dogs if they were that allergic to them.

Bitsy came back over only moments later, giving Florence a funny look. "What's up, buttercup? Did you find Groban?"

Florence shook her head. "No, though I did find out what I needed. The betting here is interesting, a little different than how the horse races are run, I believe," she said, hating the way the lie just rolled off her tongue. She truly had no idea if any it was the truth, but she did find what she was looking for at least.

"That's great! Are you still thinking about bringing your friend here?" Bitsy followed Florence's gaze and her chirpy smile faded some. "Is something the matter?"

Florence was still staring at the trailer. "I don't... I don't think so. Sorry, I think I just got confused by something." But then it hit her—she'd just seen Mary-Ann Elmhurst. It had to have been her. The yellow wool scarf stood out and suddenly Florence pictured it around Mary-Ann's neck both times she'd spoken with her.

But why in the world was she here? Was she maybe the owner of one of Lucky Marty's competition picks? Mary-Ann had mentioned her cousin being embroiled in side businesses but it looked like maybe she wasn't the only one. It took Florence a moment to realize Bitsy was knee-deep in a conversation with her and she hadn't heard a lick of it.

"The pooches are so cute but I don't think they'll let anyone in to pet them. What a shame. I wish we could keep dogs at home. My mother and father would never have it though." She shook her head, her blonde waves bouncing under her hat.

"Right. My parents are the same—I always thought it would be nice to have a cat. But Bitsy, they just let that lady in to see the dog. Why wouldn't they let you?"

"She was probably the owner. They're allowed in whenever. All of these dogs are probably worth a bunch of money. You have to be pretty loaded to be able to race them here, I bet. The same with horses over at Belmont."

Florence shoved her hands back into her pockets, pretending to empty them clean with a pout. "Well, it looks like I'm not buying my next prized champion. Rats."

15

October 24, 1925

Ginny stirred the sugar into her tea, the teaspoon clinking against the china in a slow rhythm. "He shouldn't be too much longer out on the boat. For the most part, the men are back within two months after they take off. It's a long haul and this is the time of year where they have to catch as much as they can before the dead of winter sets up. That's when things get dangerous," she said as she went to take a sip from the piping hot tea.

Florence put together the picture of Ginny's husband based on everything she'd heard so far. He was kind, sandy-haired and strong, with a quiet way about him. Even though he was a pipe fitter, he took a yearly trip with a local group of fishermen to go up the North Atlantic coast to pack their boat full of mackerel. It was a long trip, which meant Ginny was left at home, hoping and praying James made it back in one piece. Even though it brought in a good deal of money for them, it worried her.

"Do you ever get lonely? I can't imagine you looking forward to the trips out to sea," she asked, blowing the steam away from her cup of tea. The Indian Assam black tea was likely to burn her tongue if she wasn't careful.

Ginny sighed. "I do. But I try not to dwell on it so much. Besides, things have certainly taken a turn for the interesting around here as of late," she said, nudging Florence's hand with a small smile.

It had been a quiet enough morning, and after the detective's visit yesterday morning Florence wasn't sure if that was a good or bad thing.

She was still busy drawing notes in her journal when Ginny had come up with fresh milk and biscuits with butter for breakfast, more than happy to share with her.

After they'd discussed the Lucky Marty situation, Florence grew tired of thinking on it and instead started asking Ginny more questions about her. It was nice to have two friends she could look forward to spending her time with, even while missing Bernice terribly.

"What about you, Florence?" Ginny countered. "Did you have a love back in Ohio?"

At this, Florence chuckled. "Not really, no. There were a few men who were decent enough, but no one really ever caught my eye and then turned around to catch my heart as well. My friend Bernice used to laugh at me and tell me I was too big-thinking for the small-town boys. I suppose looking back, she was right. The idea of settling down with a family just because it's expected of me had never sat well with me, I'm afraid. Much to my mother's dismay."

"Big-thinking. I like that. I wouldn't consider myself that way but I could see it in you—your aunt as well."

It was hard not to smile at her. "I'll take that as a compliment coming from you. I wouldn't mind being compared to her, anyhow."

A static hiss broke through the room as the buzzer beside her bedroom door sounded. "Virginia, if you are still up there you are needed downstairs promptly. Miss Florence, you too. Quickly, now," Hamish's voice was tinny over the intercom but both women jumped up immediately, sharing the same troubled look. Hamish never called for Florence.

This could not be good.

Florence kept Ginny's dashing pace down the stairs, completely forgetting about her house slippers. She was lucky she'd thought to even put on her quilted house robe as the pair of them raced down the steps.

She wasn't sure what to expect, but the sight at the bottom of the grand staircase stopped her cold.

A man in a dark trench coat and police cap had his hands behind his back, shaking his head as two other police officers in black uniforms approached Aunt Julia slowly. A flash of silver in the shorter man's hands caught Florence's eye and she clapped her hand to her mouth as she realized what was happening.

"No!" She rushed over to the three men surrounding Aunt Julia, her eyes wide and frantic. "You can't do this! She's done nothing wrong!" she shouted.

Ginny stood at the foot at the staircase frozen in horror while Hamish quickly pulled Florence back, shaking his head at her.

But Florence wanted someone to speak up—to say something in Aunt Julia's defense! How could they stand around and let this happen?

Her cheeks burned at the sight of the men closing in around her.

"Child, hush now," Aunt Julia said in a calm, even-tempered manner. There was no anger, no unease in her tone, but the color had drained from her face. She willingly placed her hands out in front of her for the shorter officer to handcuff.

"She's a person of suspicion, Miss," the detective said, tilting his hat back. "With a body involved we can't sit around and let a potential murderer hang around without any consequence. Surely you understand that."

Aunt Julia slowly shook her head as she stared at her, her dark blue eyes narrowed. She didn't want Florence to say another word.

But Florence only heard the word *body* and her mind couldn't see how any of this was fair or reasonable. "Was someone found?" She knew no one owed her an answer but she was secretly crossing her fingers that the detective would tell her anyway.

He looked like he was maybe debating the same thing. "Yes. I suppose since this involves the lady of the house then I might mention it to you as well, Miss...?"

"Winters," she said with as much conviction as she could muster.

Thank God for small miracles.

"Right-oh. I am not sure if you're aware of the disappearance of Mrs. Adelaide Ramsey, but we turned up her missing vehicle and found a body within it." He swept his cap from his head, dusting it off.

Florence took a step back and frowned, not wanting to appear as feral and desperate as she felt.

"As the proper parties have been notified, I feel it is my duty to inform you, Mrs. Bryant, that it was Mary-Ann Elmhurst who was found along with the Ramsey car. We are still on high alert in regards to Adelaide Ramsey and her whereabouts, especially given the nature of our suspicions over Mrs. Elmhurst's cause of death." Detective Marshall placed his cap back on his head and tilted his head to the side, still looking intently at Aunt Julia. "I hadn't realized you were having houseguests over." Folding his arms across his barrel-like chest, he looked between her and Florence. "Funny you didn't mention this young lady when we asked for the statements from your house staff yesterday."

The police officers seemed to tug harder than necessary at her arms, guiding her toward the front door.

Florence hated seeing her chained like some kind of wild animal. "I came over for tea," Florence said, trying to sound as cool and collected as her aunt had. Aunt Julia hadn't wanted her to get mixed up with this business and she didn't want her to be made to look like she was hiding something.

But everyone in the room seemed to suck in their breath, leaving a vacuum of silence behind.

A strange triumphant look came over Detective Marshall's face. "Is that so?" When his gaze dropped to Florence's feet she knew she'd messed up all at once.

She was still dressed from breakfast with Ginny, barefoot with no shoes to be found, no less. And she'd completely just made a fool of herself, not only in front of Aunt Julia but, even more importantly, the detective.

Had she just helped strip her aunt of her credibility?

Florence wished the ground would open up at her feet to swallow her and her pathetic lie. No such luck, of course.

Straightening up, Aunt Julia shrugged. "I have nothing to say until my attorney arrives at the station where I'm assuming you are taking me." She turned and looked toward Florence, Hamish, and Ginny. "Please handle things while I am gone, dear. I will be back before you know it, especially once Mr. Dredd has the chance to speak with them. Everything will be ironed out and I'll be able to come back home swiftly. Keep steady, Hamish, Virginia. Nothing has changed." When she looked dead at her, the pleading in her voice to stay calm struck something deep in Florence.

Florence went to put her arm around Ginny as the police jolted Aunt Julia to move to the door, the detective lingering behind for a moment, still looking at Florence. But he eventually tipped his hat to them and Hamish rushed over to the door to shut it behind them, his eyes lined with worry.

"You heard her, ladies," he said, his old-fashioned mustache twitching with his words. "Nothing has changed. Virginia, I daresay we ought to inform Auguste of the goings-on."

Ginny quickly nodded. "A-And I have laundry to sort," she said, her voice cracking. She swallowed hard and Florence squeezed her even harder.

"It'll be all right, Ginny dear," she said softly as Hamish retreated from the room to find the chef. "I promise I will find a way to sort this out. Remember what I told you about Elm Square last night?"

Ginny's eyes clouded with confusion. "What about it?"

Florence leaned in. "Mary-Ann Elmhurst. I thought I saw her there, but she couldn't have very well been, not if she was, well, deceased. And I couldn't mention any of it just now, of course." It was something that had been burning at the back of her brain since Detective Marshall mentioned her.

"But I thought..." she trailed off. "Then it wasn't her?"

Florence frowned. "I guess not. But I'll find out if there is more to the story somehow. Poor Mary-Ann," she said as she let go of Ginny. "I can't believe she's gone. What a terrible thing... I don't see how the two can't be connected. They were cousins, there must be something more than what I'm seeing."

Ginny's light footfalls trailed out of the room as she hurried down the staff stairs by the front door to handle the laundry on the lower level. Florence felt worse seeing the stricken look on Ginny's face.

She'd mentioned how lively it had been recently at Number Seven, but Florence couldn't help but wonder if that was necessarily a good thing.

With a new determination stirring inside of her, she headed upstairs to her own room, ready to get dressed and take the next step.

16

Her notebook was smeared with ink, one of her favorite cotton middy blouses as well, as Florence scratched out several of her theories on the woman at the greyhound track, Mary-Ann's death, Adelaide's disappearance, the car crashing into the water, and how Lucky Marty was tied into it all.

None of it sounded right as she continued to reread her notes. The woman at the races last night couldn't have been Mary-Ann, that much she knew. Even if the police hadn't gotten Aunt Julia wrong in the matter, they most certainly wouldn't have messed that part up. Or at least she hoped not.

The sun porch's wide picture windows overlooked the drive leading behind the house to the carriage house's entrance, where she could make out a group of crows perched along the pitch of roof on Number Eight next door.

What was it they called a group of crows again? She vaguely studied the black birds with their black beaks open and cawing. Even from inside she would hear them plain as day.

"A murder. They're called a murder of crows," she said, wistfully thinking of how her own aunt was being dragged into a murder investigation based on the loosest of arguments. If Aunt Julia was most negatively mentioned in Adelaide Ramsey's strange letter then it stood to reason that she must've also had something to do with Adelaide's cousin's death.

She ran her hand through her hair, somewhat embarrassed at its disheveled appearance. She hadn't bothered pinning it up after watching Aunt Julia being carted off to jail only hours ago. There was no room in her heart to care.

What would happen to her? Surely the police's presence hadn't gone unnoticed in the neighborhood... which meant that the whole of St. Luke's Place would know that Julia Bryant has been arrested. It didn't matter what for, Florence realized with a sick feeling spreading through her bones. The very fact that something so shameful and scandalous had happened to the most powerful woman on the street carried weight that even she couldn't fathom.

She swung her legs up onto the settee and brought her knees up to her chin, having placed the notebook and pen and inkwell down on a nearby decorative round table.

The somber whistling caught her off guard, but then she saw him, his dark curls wild without a hat to hold them back. Benny was hosing down the drive with buckets of water before using a wide street sweep to sweep up and back along the paved space. He mopped his hair with the back of his hand, leaned the sweeper against the side of the house, and walked through the door and into the sun porch.

"Hello," he said, missing the usual bounce in his warm cadence. "Rough day, huh?"

She nodded, tightening her arms around her legs. "You can say that again."

"I know you gotta be pretty tore up with what's going on with Mrs. Bryant. But they can't keep her forever, especially when they have nothing on her."

Florence regarded Benny for a moment, her heart sinking. She didn't like how even he sounded unconvinced.

"You know, I just got back from filling up Bluebird and I overheard some cops talking about it."

Despite herself, the corner of her mouth twitched. "Did you just call the car Bluebird?"

Benny went to open his mouth but looked as though he thought better of it. The sheepish grin said it all. "As I was *saying*... I took the car to the gasoline pump. When I hopped out to pay the man to fill the tank, a couple of off-duty police officers were busy clapping their traps at the next pump over. One of them was telling the other one how they think they got the suspect for the death of that rich lady on Berker Street."

Florence's blood ran cold. "They were talking about Aunt Julia."

He nodded. "Yes, but that wasn't all. It sounds like the word is getting around, and not only about Mrs. Bryant but about how they think Mary-Ann Elmhurst was killed."

Taking a deep breath, Florence waited a beat. "And what did they say?"

There was a look of regret that crossed Benny's usually upbeat expression. "It isn't pretty. The police went to Mary-Ann's home and found a large candlestick covered in blood somewhere inside. They think she was bludgeoned to death before someone tried to dump her in the East River. They're not sure if the car thing was intentional or not, though."

A pin-pricking swept over Florence's skin in a slow wave of glaring discomfort. She felt sick at the very thought. "Bludgeoned to death? What an absolutely heartless and brutal way to die!"

"I know. Like I said, it's not pretty," Benny said, gauging her reaction.

"I think horrifying might fit better," she choked out, slowly straightening her legs out. "Poor Mary-Ann. I can't imagine anyone doing such a thing. And in her own house, no less. Just when you think you're safe..." Chills inched up her spine.

"Any more theories on what's going on? Weren't you talking about the racetracks before?" he asked.

It all came out like a flood, and she told him everything from where she'd left off the last time they talked.

"Who had the car if Adelaide was missing and so was the car? I just don't get how this all fits together."

Benny, who was now sitting on the edge of an overstuffed chintz armchair, folded his hands out in front of him, his elbows on his knees. "Huh."

"And not to mention I just talked to Mary-Ann Elmhurst. Right after the church service this past Sunday, in fact!"

Benny nodded. "I remember seeing the two of you, yeah."

"Right. I really wish I knew when she'd officially died. Was it right after I'd spoken to her? Later that night? Or more recently?" Florence groaned, her head dropping back against the soft cushion of the settee. "I'd hate to think I could've prevented any of it from happening to her..."

His posture went rigid as he sat straight up. "No, Florence. You can't think like that. You'll drive yourself crazy. There's nothing you could've done without potentially putting yourself in danger."

She blew a long strand of wavy hair from her face and sat back up to face him. "Logically that makes sense, but it's hard not to let my mind wander..."

Why was it that Adelaide was the one missing, that it was Adelaide's car found in the water, and yet Adelaide was nowhere to be found while her cousin was the one dead inside of the car? It was as if there was a giant puzzle piece glaringly missing from the rest.

"You look like you've already got something brewing in your head," he said as he folded his arms across his chest.

She bit her lip. "That obvious, huh? I was only thinking... well, I don't really know. I want to figure out where I should take my next step. If Adelaide isn't missing and she hasn't been done in the same way as Mary-Ann was, then something else is going on and it's quite possible the police have no idea. Especially since I know about Lucky Marty and they don't... sort of."

"If Mrs. Ramsey isn't missing, then she might have other plans for herself. And that dog has to be worth a pretty penny if he's hers, or if he's the one her dog is racing against. Either way you're right, it's definitely fishy," Benny agreed. "I don't think you'll get much information outside of the racetrack, though."

She was afraid he'd say that, but of course he was only being truthful. An underground greyhound racing enterprise wasn't something people would likely be talking about, especially in polite society. "No, I don't suppose I will. Unless..." She raised a brow at Benny. "If I can get in and watch the next race myself. The guys at the track mentioned it being double winnings the day after tomorrow. If anything of importance is going to happen, it'll be then."

While she was able to get in the first time around thanks to Bitsy's quick thinking and way with words, Florence was doubtful she could pull off anything of the sort, and she didn't want to bring Bitsy into it again. Especially since she'd been keeping the whole truth from her.

The corners of Benny's eyes crinkled in a way that Florence found endearing when he smiled. "Nothing much is going to happen between now and whenever the police let Mrs. Bryant come home. I doubt it will be very long, but in the meantime... we could make ourselves useful."

"Oh?"

He nodded and gave her a quick salute. "As your temporary partner in crime, I think I know a way into Elm Square Men's Club. But... you'll have to trust me."

Florence slowly rose. The last thing she wanted was for Benny to compromise himself or his position at the house. "Are you sure you want to do this?"

"I wouldn't offer if I wasn't."

She looked him over one good time, her attention all over the place at once somehow. "Then I trust you."

OCTOBER 26, 1925

"I TAKE IT ALL BACK. I don't trust you."

Florence leaned back against the seat of the Buick, peering through the windows to the Elm Square Men's Club. Something about it against the nighttime skyline felt darker than before. Not darker, but sinister.

Benny pulled to a stop at the front where a valet was waiting for him to pull up. "You don't mean that."

She took in the crooked smile and folded her arms underneath the nicest coat she could find in her closet. "I could."

"Come on. Let's get out of here before the guy gets suspicious," he said, opening the door to hop out and help Florence out of the passenger cab. "There you are, darling." With a swipe from the driver's compartment, he placed a bowler hat on his head and took her hand. "I've heard the race is pretty tight tonight," he said, winking at the valet before tossing him the keys.

Florence's face flushed as the pair of them walked up the steps, trailing after other wealthy folks. This all felt like too much to her. Benny had suggested they take on the roles of a married couple, where hopefully he could play it off for them to slip through mostly unnoticed. Since she already knew how to reach the racetrack, that was the only thing holding them back.

But Florence recalled the cantankerous man from before. She didn't think it would be quite that easy. Then again, it was her only real shot at getting in because she certainly wouldn't be let in without a man at her side this time.

Everyone was busy chattering away as they all waited to be checked in at the front desk. Despite the whole racing gig being supposedly underground, most people talked quite openly about the races tonight.

"I don't know, Roger. Heaven's Angel was looking a little devilish tonight, if you know what I mean," a man with an unlit cigar said, waggling his thick eyebrows at his companion.

The other gentleman—Roger, she assumed—shook his head. "I don't get it."

Right behind them was an older couple in matching his-and-hers argyle golf outfits. They stared straight ahead with absolutely blank expressions.

"Talk about a poker face," Benny leaned in, whispering under his breath. He nodded his chin toward the couple and Florence bit her lip to keep from giggling.

When it got to be their turn, Florence wasn't sure whether to be relieved by the absence of the man from yesterday or disgusted by the way the new guy looked her up and down like a dog hankering for a bone. Benny pulled her arm to encircle his, the man glancing down at where Benny's upper arm muscles flexed and strained against his suit.

The man narrowed his beady eyes at Benny. "Are you a member here? Because I don't buy it."

Florence frowned. This wasn't going to work... they were going to have to think of another plan—another way in without anyone seeing them...

"Of course not, sir. I work here as a, uh, custodian," Benny said, flashing an easy but polite smile at the man. "The boss has been extra pleased with my uh, work ethic, and invited me to come out for a night this week." He laughed. "Who knew? So I'm bringing my little lady in for a little surprise tonight. She goes gaga over the mutts, I tell ya."

All she could do was pray he would buy it.

The man looked between the two of them again and shook his head, muttering something she couldn't quite make out. "All right. You're in. Just make sure you keep to the ground and don't go sitting in the stands. I'm sure the boss explained it to all you janitors."

If this was meant to intimidate Benny it didn't work, and he gave a brief nod and thanked him. "Yes, sir. Understood."

When they were finally halfway down the hallway that led to the Private Personnel Only door, she paused. They let a couple of people past and she waited until the door had shut behind them.

"What was all that about? That man, he was so... so rude to you!" Now that she thought about it, a sort of quiet rage bubbled up under her skin. Florence didn't lose her temper easily, but when she did it was not pretty.

Benny just shrugged. "I guess I was fooling myself into thinking they'd buy a guy like me as a member of this hoity-toity establishment. I should've gone with the chauffeur uniform and just told him I was escorting you to your husband or something."

She frowned. "But I don't understand. You're dressed to kill, and you're driving around that expensive car."

Benny stared at her before they separated to let more people past. "Florence... they don't let guys like me into places like this. Unless we're cleaning toilets or fixing pipes or something, you know? We don't fit in. I just forgot."

He held his hand alongside hers and it slowly sunk in, piercing this veil that she hadn't realized was there between the two of them. Shame flooded through her.

"Oh." It was all she could manage to say as she pulled the too-hot gauzy scarf from around her neck.

"Nah, don't worry about it. Let's get you downstairs so you can do your investigating," he said good-naturedly as if nothing had happened. "Come on."

She sighed and followed after him, still not likely to forget the rude man or his insinuations.

Downstairs was not as it was before. Sure, the room itself was nearly the same but the energy in the room, the very feeling of it, was completely different.

The anticipation, the cheers and shouts and laughing as people shuffled around to their respective places—all of it was new. Over the intercom the race times were being announced and it echoed like a wind in a cave.

"Huh. This is pretty exciting, isn't it? If you're into that sort of thing," Benny said as they wound their way over to the stands. Just as the man warned him, Benny did not try and find seats for them there, but rather, led Florence over to stand not far from where the dog kennels were.

This way they'd have a better look at what might be going on behind the scenes, he'd already explained.

"It's most certainly not my thing. But I suppose there is a sort of strange liveliness here I wasn't really expecting."

Benny smiled, pointing to the kennel behind them. "My cousin lives on a farm upstate. Has something like fifty acres to himself. He's a dog kind of guy—has three of them and a bunch of animals to help work the place over. A real farmer type, believe it or not. I've always wanted to go visit him up there in Ellicottville. I bet he'd love to have those guys back there. Nobody should be cooped up for nothing in return."

She had to hand it to Benny, he was absolutely right.

A handful of people passed by; two of the men stopped as they slipped around the stands. They were close enough to hear but couldn't see Florence or Benny from where they were standing. She suddenly felt nervous. Nothing about this place felt particularly safe, though she was thankful for Benny's presence.

Someone cleared their throat. "The champ? Nah, not tonight, pal. You're on. I've got thirty clams on the ringer."

"You're on, chump. Lucky Marty's been on fire for months now. Nothing's holding him back tonight. Lady Luck will be on his side… and mine," the other man wheezed. "Why are you betting on the ringer?"

But the other man only laughed. "Let's blouse. We need to find our seats before the shows really begin."

After their footsteps retreated, Benny leaned around the corner to double-check and make sure they'd gone. There was something about his expression that worried Florence.

"What is it?" she asked.

"I think it's been compromised." He frowned as the both of them gazed in the direction of the kennels.

"Compromised?"

"The house is rigged," he hissed by her ear. "That's what I mean."

She watched the people finish filling in the stands on the left, the roar of the crowd getting louder and louder as they packed into their seats. "As in... they know who's the winner? But how can they do that?"

Surely they couldn't plan something like that with animals. She'd heard of card games and slot machines being rigged to favor the house, but how could you control how fast an animal runs?

Benny pulled his bowler hat off to reveal his mess of black curls. "I don't know. But I'm telling you, something's up. That's why the guy said that just now. I could see it in his face. He knows something and I think it's about Lucky Marty." He drew in a deep breath, looking all around them before continuing. "The bets are high on his side as it is, right? So imagine knowing that a sure thing that everyone else is betting on is going to lose. It takes your chance of winning and greatly increases it. If you do happen to hit it, then you've really hit it against the poor fools who didn't. Now take that and double it—it's double winnings night and folks are looking to make the biggest cash grab they can. If you happen to hit the winner in a race like this?"

Benny shot his hand way up as if it were a plane taking off. "Sky-high. I wouldn't be surprised if something shady was going off."

That reminded her... "One of the guys did say something like that. That they had to keep an eye out because it was double winnings night and people got desperate."

"Exactly. But the question is this... why isn't Lucky Marty winning tonight?"

She looked out over the racetrack that had been freshly recovered. "And who is?"

17

"Owners, please have your runners to the pit. We are up on the first race of the evening, nine o'clock sharp; please have your runners to the pit in the next five minutes," a booming voiced echoed throughout the racetrack.

More lights overhead and circling the track burst to life. Florence couldn't quite understand how people found any of this enjoyable, but it was very clear that the people gathered here did. Several of them in the stands let out loud whoops and hollers. The most excitement you'd find in Jebediah, Ohio, was when the school's marching band put on their annual parade down the main drag of town.

She searched the stands, wondering if she might see the woman from the other night. There were easily two hundred people spread throughout the stands, and Florence sighed at the impossibility of finding someone she hadn't even properly seen to begin with.

"According to the sign over there, Lucky Marty's race is the third one in. Nine thirty. Now, are we looking for something in particular here, or...?" Benny asked.

Florence fanned herself—the lights overhead really put out some heat. "Honestly, I think the best thing would be to find out who owns him first. I don't know the connection between him and Adelaide and Mary-Ann, but something's telling me I'm on the right path. I just wish I knew why."

Trusting her gut was something Florence rarely ever thought twice about, but these were unusual circumstances. If she got it wrong then she might miss her chance to help prove Aunt Julia innocent of whatever erroneous charges the police were trying to hold her on. Either way, she needed to think fast.

"Let's take a look closer back this way. The woman could be back here; I mean, she was when I saw her before," she said, gesturing to the space behind the stands. They weren't far from the smaller building she'd accidentally leaned against. Bitsy hadn't seemed to notice the other night, thankfully.

The two of them wove through the smaller crowd of people who were trying to get glimpses of the dogs, including some photographers who tried bypassing several men holding the line.

One of them had the camera knocked out of his hand by the tallest of the security detail, and when it crashed to the ground, the photographer screeched. "Do you know how much that thing cost me?"

The huge man towered over the rest of them and cracked his knuckles, the strength in his gesture sending shockwaves through the rest of the photographers.

"Buddy, that thing is gonna cost you your life if you don't scram," one man hissed at him, thumbing toward the huge guy who'd shoved him. "That's one of Old Nick's guys. Get outta here before you regret it."

Quickly scooping his trashed camera, the man streaked out of there without another word.

"Never a dull moment," Benny said as he leaned in toward Florence.

She nodded but kept an eye on both the security men and the kennels behind them. A secret gambling establishment run by a gang of sorts was probably the last place you'd want to start taking pictures, but what did she know?

Despite the scene, not much else happened before the announcer welcomed and thanked everyone for coming out tonight. He rattled off the race times and the dogs racing—there would be a total of six races tonight—and reminded everyone to check in with their slips to collect their winnings. "No funny business," he'd said in a lighthearted way though his tone suggested he truly meant it.

Florence noticed that there'd been no official name given to the race organization or the place, and a frown slid down her mouth. Even though she was here willingly, she suddenly wondered if it was the smart thing to do.

But she didn't have much time to dwell on it as the first race was set up, the dogs being put in their respective pit lanes. The crowd roared to life when the gunshot cracked through the air, piercing the night. A green light flashed at the beginning of the track where a fake rabbit sped off along a metal rail, enticing the dogs to chase after it.

Plenty of onlookers were cheering on their picks, others were watching fiercely. Everyone was up out of their seats, unable to hold back their excitement.

The quarter-mile track seemed like it took the dogs a blink of an eye to cover, and when the cream-colored dog cleverly named Walkabout won the race, it was as though the room exploded. Cheers and screams filled the air, boos and worse too. Florence fought the urge to plug her ears from all of the noise.

But Benny just laughed, shaking his head as some of it died out.

Florence glanced back behind them at the kennels where the rest of the dogs were being kept. The same pretty fawn-and-white dog she'd seen before was sniffing along the edges of the kennel, his long snout poking through the chain links. She smiled and wondered again about his name. The charcoal gray one with the green and gold tags was still in the kennel too. So Lucky Marty might have still been in the mix after all.

"They're cute, huh?" Benny's voice pulled her back into the present.

"Hmm? Oh, yes. Very much."

The second race went just as the first, right at quarter past and they shot off like fireworks, making a mad dash around the track. This time Florence watched as the three battling for the lead took the last turn.

They were neck and neck until one of them slowed a hair and the other two shot past the finish line at the exact same moment, much to the jeers of the crowd. No one liked a close finish when there was no real way to see the winner. Florence knew that even with the film camera installed at the finish line, the race would probably be too close to call.

"What happens now?" she asked Benny, her eyes still trained on the two dogs as a man and woman, whom she assumed to be the dogs' owners, came out to talk to the men down at the finish line.

"I don't know but I don't think it's going to be a simple shaking of hands, if that's what you mean." His brows knitted together as he looked at her. "Look alive. Lucky Marty's up next."

The minutes between the second and third races felt like they dragged on forever. An anxious sort of energy hovered over her, not quite clinging but ready to grab her at any moment.

She searched the group of people around the dogs who were gearing them up to race. The gray dog was first out of the gate, after his green-and-gold collar was slipped from his neck and the race number strapped around his smooth and barrel-like body. Number eight. Florence was surprised when he was walked over to the innermost lane and shuttered inside the pit cage with the white number painted over it.

Heaven's Angel. She hadn't pictured that dog a kind of angel at all, but her attention was torn clean away when the fawn-and-white dog, the very same one she'd been looking at, pranced over to the number seven lane, his tongue lolling out.

She couldn't believe it. "Benny, look! It's Lucky Marty!" He was being escorted by one of the pit crew men instead of his owner.

Benny watched too, his concentration focused on the dog. "That can't be his owner. They wouldn't let one of their own race the dogs."

"I was thinking the same thing. So his owner seems to be absent. Interesting, that." She scanned the stands again but there was still no one that stood out in a yellow scarf and large hat. And now that Florence thought harder about it, she was surprised she hadn't realized it before.

The woman had been patting Lucky Marty the other night after all! So she was right in thinking there was something odd going on, but she hardly had time to think more on it when the third shot of the night rang out and the dogs were let loose.

Lucky Marty was like a blur compared to the other dogs, his paws pounding the dirt so hard it was as if he were flying, not running. When he came up on the last stretch, Florence's heart fluttered.

It would come down to this. Was Benny right? He tensed next to her and Lucky Marty skirted the corner.

Later, she would still be unable to point out the moment when Lucky Marty slowed down. It all happened so fast that when the other two dogs shot past him, she was still in shock that it was actually happening.

The dog on the outside, Heaven's Angel, looked a foot or so ahead of the dog wearing the number six around its body. A bright light seemed to flash off the side of the finish line, and Heaven's Angel, visibly stunned, crossed the checkered line a hair behind number six.

Lucky Marty was third, and Florence was sure she would've known he'd lost the race even if she hadn't been watching, with the way everyone cried foul.

"Hairpin Sally, the winner of the nine thirty race!" the announcer called out.

People were stomping, some pushing their way down the stands. Florence wasn't sure what *she* was expecting but it was very clear that no one had been expecting Lucky Marty to lose, much less come in third. The anger in the huge room was nearly palpable.

Benny tugged at her sleeve. "Florence, did you see that?"

She tilted her head to better hear him over the noise. "Sorry?"

"The light. Did you see that light? At the finish line?"

"The green light?"

But he shook his head. "No, the other one. The green light went off when number six crossed, but before that. There was a small flash of light when number eight took the lead."

But hadn't that been just a bulb blinking, or maybe the light hitting someone's jewelry or... she blinked. "Heaven's Angel was in the lead and the light must have blinded him for a moment, just enough time..."

"...For number six to pull ahead right at the finish line," he continued, folding his arms across his chest. "There's no way that's a coincidence."

"There are no coincidences. And we can't be the only people who noticed, either." She gazed at the spot where they'd seen the flash of light, more questions piling up in her mind.

The big straw hat was the first thing she noticed, but then when she caught sight of the thick yellow wool scarf around the woman's neck, she gasped. "Oh my—Benny, it's the woman!"

The woman was in the same outfit as before, and was busy very obviously trying to slink past others and away from the finish line where too many people were starting to gather.

"Come on!" Florence said, already a few steps ahead of him. "Let's follow her."

"Florence, wait up! Hey!"

While she was struggling to keep her eyes on the woman, her mind had no trouble sifting through everything again, racing not unlike the dogs on the track.

The woman's scarf had been what drew her attention, especially since she was certain it was the very same one Mary-Ann had. As Adelaide had put it, it looked very itchy and was ugly as sin. It would be hard to find one like it, though Florence supposed it wasn't out of the question.

Speaking of itchy, Adelaide had seemed irritated by the scarf, but then again so had Aunt Julia so that hardly meant... The woman had a sneezing fit right around the corner the other night, hadn't she?

Lucky Marty was this woman's dog, she just knew he was. She recalled the way the woman had scratched and patted the dog before. But that led to another question and she couldn't stop rolling through them no matter the noise or push of people all around her.

Adelaide had gone missing but had somehow managed to leave that scathing letter about Aunt Julia, and Mary-Ann hadn't seemed that bothered by her own cousin's disappearance. Florence had figured that maybe there was something else going on there but when the news of Mary-Ann's death came about, it had fallen to the wayside and all she could think of was how terrible she felt.

Could it be? Could Adelaide be Lucky Marty's owner? Was she the woman in the hat and scarf? But then why was she in hiding? And if she was, then certainly she would've pulled her dog from the racing lineup.

Benny caught up with her and put his hand on her shoulder, his dark eyes concerned. "Where are you running off to, exactly? We have to stay together or else I won't know where to find you. I don't think you want to be hoofing it back to Number Seven."

"I think I know who that woman is," she said, irritated that she'd finally lost sight of her. "But I don't understand any of it, Benny, I really don't."

He nodded. "All right, you stay here. There's something I want to check out really quick but I'll be right back, okay? I mean it. Stay put."

"This is hardly the time—"

"Stay. Put. I told you to trust me, right?"

Florence looked up and for the first time since they'd been in the car, she really saw him. The dark curls at the nape of his neck and curling out from under his bowler hat. The way tiny flecks of dark brown circled around his pupils. She hadn't noticed that before.

"Yes, yes," she said, turning away before she blushed and more.

He watched her for a moment, searching her eyes. "All right. Be right back." He gave her a nod and off he went, though she had no clue as to where he was going.

And then she saw the big straw hat again and without thinking, she was moving.

Benny would understand.

18

Florence hadn't realized there was a whole back area to the indoor track arena until she was gunning for it after the mysterious woman whom she was already half-convinced was Adelaide Ramsey herself.

Sweat clung to her skin under the lights, the heavy coat and her felt cloche more of a hindrance than help at this point. But she kept pushing through the surge of people, dead set on keeping an eye on the woman.

All around people were giving their half-cocked opinions on the races, eating concession snacks and knocking back what had to be beer. The aroma of Cracker Jack and Coca-Cola filled the air and she couldn't help but think of how ironic it was to see these illegal races treated like they were the next Cincinnati Reds game. Old Nick really must have had an understanding with the New York City Police because otherwise, she couldn't understand how an event like this could go unnoticed by the law.

"There you are," Florence mumbled under her breath, losing track of the woman for just a split-second before her hat gave her away. The woman slipped in between two wooden beams in front of the long line at the concession stand, heading into a side hallway.

After the snack stand, the crowd thinned out considerably. She was thinking of shucking her coat but something held her back. If—and it was a big if—she needed to be quick on her feet then it made more sense just to keep it on than have to fold the puffy thing over her arm.

The wide hallway was poorly lit compared to the rest of the space, the other corridors leading off from it not much better.

She kept a pace that set her a few people behind the woman until she disappeared down another hallway where no one bothered following. Florence edged up to it and peeked around.

The hem of the woman's coat could be seen just as she walked into the only door Florence could see. Was that a way out, perhaps?

Something shoved up against her shoulder and she nearly smacked her head into the painted cinder block wall as the man passed by her, mumbling his apologies. Another man in a white fedora and pinstripe suit followed, tipping his hat at her before rounding the same corner.

She didn't get the chance to see the taller man's face until he walked into the same room as the woman and she raised a brow as soon as she realized who he was.

The security team—the man who'd shoved the photographer down and broken his camera. He nearly hit the threshold of the door walking into the room, and the other man, the one in the hat, looked vaguely familiar though she was certain she'd never seen his face before.

I've seen him around... looks sorta like Buster Keaton. Why?

This must have been Bill Groban! The very guy she was trying to find the last time she was here and there he went, trailing after the woman.

Florence suddenly felt like she was walking in quicksand, unable to move as fast as she wanted to. The way both the security guy and Bill Groban carried themselves as they went through the door had left a sinking feeling deep in her bones. There was a glint in their eyes and a tensing of their fists at their sides that she didn't like.

An alarm went off in her head. Stay back. This is not safe.

No wonder she was having a hard time moving. Florence glanced back over her shoulder, glad to see at least a few people walking nearby. This must have been the way everyone brought in their dogs and equipment, she figured. If something bad were to happen then surely someone would hear.

It was all she could hope for as she swallowed hard and followed after the woman and the men.

There were precisely two things that jumped out to Florence as she crept up to the doorway, sweeping her hat from her head.

One, the room was a small storage room of sorts. Lockers and cubbies lined most of it, with broken chairs and a large trash can taking up space in the middle of the floor.

And two, the woman was tiny in comparison as Bill Groban and the beefed-up security guy approached her. When she spun around, she had a large tote bag hanging from her shoulder and a small slip of paper clutched in her other hand.

At first glance, Florence hoped that she was walking in on some kind of agreed-to rendezvous, where the meetup between them was planned ahead of time. Maybe the other woman won big and was giving them a cut. Maybe they were helping her in some other way even.

But the moment the woman fumbled and backed herself into a corner, Florence's heart dropped. This was something else entirely.

An interrogation.

Bill carefully tipped his hat to the woman, no sign of politeness anywhere to be seen. "Miss. My associate Ulysses and I would like to have a little chat with you before you take off."

Florence bit her lip.

"Oh?" the woman squeaked, quickly stuffing the paper into a pocket. But Bill just closed the space between them to pluck the paper from that pocket and hold it up.

"Huh. This is a mighty big winning slip you got here. One hundred thousand clams on a third-ranked dog—on double winnings night, no less. That's some luck," he said, handing the paper over to Ulysses who grunted and tucked the betting slip into his own jacket.

The woman adjusted the round sunglasses on her face, sticking her chin in the air. "Is it a crime to have good luck?"

"Nah, but that's not what's going on here, now is it?" Bill Groban flexed his hand at his side, his thick eyebrows knitting together as he lowered his voice. "Lady, I don't know how you knew the champ was going down tonight, but you better spill it. You know something, I know you do," Bill said, his finger in her face. "You know his owner, don't you? Was she making him run heavy? Feeding him too much?"

The woman quickly shook her head and tried to sidestep him but Ulysses took one step to easily put his large frame in front of her to block her. There was a mildly amused smile on his face that made Florence's stomach roil.

"I didn't... I didn't do anything!" The woman tried yet again to make a mad dash for it, nearly squeezing past before Ulysses grabbed for her and pulled her back. She slammed against the closed lockers, crying out in fear.

Florence clutched at her coat, clapping her mouth with her hand and whirling away from the doorway for a moment, hoping no one heard her. She needed to find help somewhere—whoever this woman was, no matter if she was Adelaide, a criminal, or someone else, no one deserved to be treated this way.

"Down, boy," Bill growled at the bigger man, shaking his head. "And you," he said as he turned back toward the woman. "Don't think I didn't see your little trick with the light. What, you thought you could get away with something like that? What did you use? A flashlight? A mirror? Answer me!"

She only pulled the tote bag tighter across her shoulder. "Please let me past, I haven't done any of those things."

With a flick of his wrist, Bill Groban whipped the hat from the woman's head. "Huh. I didn't take you for a coward." She tried to scamper backward but she wasn't fast enough and he swiped her sunglasses, too.

Standing there with Mary-Ann's itchy wool scarf still wrapped tightly around her neck, an angry and terrified Adelaide Ramsey scowled at the men. "Give me those back!"

"You?" The incredulity in his voice was genuine. While Florence was shocked to see she was actually right, he truly had no idea.

"You bet against your own dog?" His bark of a laugh would've fit right in at the kennels. "I guess I see why you went missing. I should've known something screwy was going on when they found your cousin dead in the river. Bet you didn't know she let it slip that you were thinking of taking the dog to Florida. Nice sunny beaches and two hundred thousand to rest easy on, eh? Ulysses, get a look at this broad!"

Both men laughed, but there was zero humor in the room. The hair on Florence's arms stood up even under the heavy coat.

"You know, I thought she mentioned something about betting this week. Mary-Ann's been awfully lonely since her poor husband died in the war, ain't that right? She was around while you were doing your whole woman pageantry crap you do to try and make yourself feel important. Like someone gives a crap." Bill put his hands at his hips, a cruel smile pulling his face taut. "She talked, your cousin did. Is that why she's dead? Did she get in your way, Mrs. Ramsey?"

In a move that absolutely astounded Florence, Adelaide copied Bill Groban, putting her hands at her hips. "She always was such a bigmouth. I told her about that in strict confidence."

Oh no. The image of a large, bloodied candlestick loomed in Florence's mind. She'd only just talked to Mary-Ann…

Mary-Ann must have known Adelaide's plans to skip town with Lucky Marty and the money... Maybe Adelaide knew she wouldn't keep silent, so *she* decided to silence her.

There was a silent beat before both men roared with laughter, this time true laughter, ending with Bill Groban slapping his thigh.

"Well I'll be, Mrs. Ramsey! Looks like you got it all figured out. Except the part where I find out you're stealing from me. Probably should've thought out your little stowaway number some more. Ulysses?"

The man towered over her and brought his hands up—

"Wait!" Florence blurted out as she rushed in, cheeks burning, eyes wide. "Don't hurt her!" Something inside her shrieked, begging her to run while she still could.

But Florence couldn't just let them do... whatever they were about to do to Adelaide. Killer or not.

Bill Groban took a step back, his eyes flicking over to her. He looked like the devil negotiating his next deal. "Take a hike, lady. You don't want no part of this."

Ulysses yanked at Adelaide's arms, dragging her back away from the corner.

Florence drew in a shaky breath. "I said don't hurt her." And she knew. She knew then and there that she wasn't leaving this room. Whatever else happened, well, at least she tried to save the woman's life. Even if she didn't necessarily deserve it.

"Yeah, listen to the girl," Adelaide screeched, trying to pry her way out of Ulysses' iron grip.

If there had been any amusement in his face, it died off, and

Bill Groban pointed at her. She could practically see the venom dripping from his words. "You're going to regret not minding your own business, broad."

His legs were longer than she judged and he was crossing the space between them in wide strides. Without thinking, she grabbed the nearest broken chair and held it up, keeping her distance.

"Stay back. Let her go and I won't scream," she said, her voice wavering. A white-hot panic was setting in and she wasn't sure of her next move just yet. She wasn't even sure how she managed to get herself into this position in the first place.

Because curiosity killed the cat, and no one's more curious than you, doll! Bernice's voice floated in Florence's head.

Bill bared his teeth at her and made a grab for the chair, yanking at one mangled leg before it broke clean off. Florence screamed, desperate to keep an eye on Adelaide and keep Bill away from her.

He lunged forward again and this time wrenched the flimsy chair from her grasp, Florence nearly losing her balance from the momentum. She scuttled backward, torn between diving out the door or staying in the room.

He snatched at her coat and shoved her out the door, deciding for her. As her head thwacked against the concrete wall, no longer padded by her hat, she blinked and watched him slam the door to the room shut.

Her head was exploding, surely it was. Fuzzy spaces of black formed along the seams of her vision, and she swore she heard a train tearing through the hallway. Or maybe it was the blood rushing to her head. She couldn't seem to shake the noise, and when she went to stand, she found that everything turned sideways.

She groaned, her stomach churning.

Somewhere down the hallway, feet were pounding the floor. "Florence? Florence!"

The floor was cold against her cheek and suddenly a pair of shiny loafers appeared by her face, arms pulling at her, cradling her.

"Ow," she moaned, reaching up to feel the back of her head. She was sure she'd find a macabre sight when she pulled her hand back but luckily she wasn't bleeding. Not on the outside, anyway.

It took her a moment to realize it was Benny holding her. Benny was looking at her expectantly, brushing the hair from her face.

"Can you hear me? Florence?"

She tried to nod but it did not work and she groaned. Her mouth was dry but she had to say something somehow. "Adelaide. It's her, she... she's the one. She killed her, and now they have her. Groban, he..." she trailed off, the room still spinning around her. "In there." She couldn't tell him just where *there* was, but the door was being busted in by someone and Benny was scooping her up and they were moving.

She closed her eyes, unable to handle all of the moving and the lights as they went by overhead.

"Stay awake, you hear me? Don't go passing out on me just yet, *tesoro*."

"I'll... I'll try," she said softly, surprised when the words came out.

But they flickered just like the world around her.

19

A COLD SWEAT broke out over her head but she jolted awake, not even realizing she was asleep to begin with. Something burned at the inside of her nose and she blinked away the tears welling up in her eyes.

"What on earth was that?" She choked on the acrid taste of whatever it was on her tongue.

"Sorry, Miss. Smelling salts," the man in the white uniform said, pulling out some kind of light—a flashlight—to check her eyes. "Follow the light, please."

Florence blinked at the brightness but did as she was told, relieved when the light went out with a click. Where was she? The walls were painted concrete blocks, leading to a concession stand she could just make out at the end of this hallway.

She was still at the Elm Square Men's Club, it appeared.

"Thanks, doc. Is she okay to go or should I take her to the hospital? She looked like she hit her head good. Maybe she should have one of those X-rays." Benny. Benny was here with her and she slowly started remembering what was happening.

"Adelaide! They took her!" she said, struggling to stand up. She was still a little woozy, she was disappointed to find.

"Whoa, whoa. Just sit down for a minute, Florence. Let the doctor finish looking at you," he said, putting his hand on her shoulder.

She looked at him, trying to gain enough strength to put it all together again. "Where is Adelaide Ramsey?"

At this, Benny smiled and the churning in her stomach lessened. "Apprehended by the police. You'll never believe it, though."

"Why's that?" She rubbed at her nose and thanked the doctor for handing her a handkerchief.

Benny ran his hand through his thick hair, his bowler hat gone. "We picked one heck of a night to come out, I tell you. I noticed a friend of mine in the mix of people after the third race, when you were gung-ho in following the woman. Sorry, Mrs. Ramsey. Anyway, that's where I went, to flag him down and see what he was doing here. And then you went on about your business, even after I asked you to stay put," he added, raising a brow at her.

She sniffed. "Well, it was hardly the time for a social call."

"My friend's presence was more than a little coincidence. You see, it was my cousin actually, an officer for the good ol' NYPD. Sorry, the New York Police Department, for you out-of-towners." He grinned. "I didn't expect to see him here for sure, and then he told me what was really going on. Apparently it was a sting operation, and we just walked right into the middle of it."

This time she did stand up, albeit slowly. A sting operation? Wasn't that something they did to bust up the mafia and gangs? She bit her lip and nodded. "Right. Old Nick?"

"Actually, he's managed to keep his hands clean this time. It was Bill Groban they were aiming for. And thanks to you, they got him."

"No. I had nothing to do with it—Adelaide was in there and I just couldn't stand by... they were going to kill her. I'm sure of it," she said, instantly regretting shaking her head. No, she needed to stand still or this headache would knock her flat on her rear end again.

Benny reached out and put his hand on her arm. "They found him and that goon of his thanks to you. You sent 'em right in and they found the three of them before Groban and his guy had a chance to do anything."

She looked down at him, still not understanding. "And Adelaide? What did they do with her?"

"I guess she thought you told them everything already and confessed to killing her cousin. My cousin Emiliano said it was pretty funny to see the look on her face when she realized none of them had any idea what she was talking about at first."

Florence pictured Adelaide rattling on, admitting her terrible secrets, only to find that she was really just telling on herself. It couldn't undo what Adelaide had done to Mary-Ann, but it filled a small satisfaction in her somewhere. "Good riddance. I hope they lock her up and throw away the key."

October 27, 1925

THE NIGHT BLED into day at some point, and Florence never thought she'd be so glad to be back in her own bed again. The silky sheets felt like her saving grace as she crashed down on them. She heaved a great big sigh and wrapped her arms around herself, ready for the sweet surrender of sleep.

That was, until the door buzzer went off. "Miss Winters? She's back!" Ginny said over the tinny intercom.

Florence was downstairs in a flash—well, as quickly as she could, still nursing a wretched headache the doctor who'd come by earlier said was normal. But when she got down to the grand room, she drew in a choked sob and rushed at Aunt Julia with all her might, throwing her arms around her as if she were her mother after one of their bad fights.

"Oh, Auntie, I'm so glad you're home," she said, not caring if everyone was staring or not. "I was so worried about you."

She smiled as Aunt Julia's arms circled around her, holding her close. She wasn't sure if she was the hugging type, but if she wasn't, she didn't let on.

"Florence, dear. You be careful now, I don't want you to overexert yourself after that nasty hit to the head," she said, pulling away. The genuine tired smile on her face gave Florence an overwhelming sense of peace. She was home, which meant the police had let her go.

"And the charges? They dropped them?" she asked softly, standing back to give her some room.

Aunt Julia nodded, straightening up. "Of course. Once they realized their mistake and finally let me call Mr. Dredd, we tied everything up in a nice pretty bow. They'll not be banging on this door for any type of foolishness again, believe you me."

Hamish, whom Florence had only just registered was standing in the vestibule, took Aunt Julia's coat. "You are most correct about that, Missus. They'll be met with a mean old Scot who'll have none of it."

For the first time since she'd met the man, she witnessed him smile in a fierce, intimidating sort of way that one could use to scare small children.

Ginny was silently crying off to the side, and dabbed at her face with her apron. "Missus, we're so glad you've come home. It hasn't been the same without you."

Aunt Julia went over to her and gave her a quick and grateful squeeze. "It is all sorted now, Virginia dear. You'll let your mother know?"

Ginny nodded with a watery smile. "Of course."

"And I will be requesting an appropriate feast from Auguste for all of us. You three as well," Aunt Julia said, nodding to Ginny, then Hamish, and Benny, who had just come in, his driver's cap slightly askew.

The three house staff shared grateful smiles, or at least Ginny and Benny did. Hamish appeared more scandalized than anything.

Sneaky dashed out past Florence's feet and wove a path in and around Aunt Julia's feet, mewling like some little kitten.

When Aunt Julia picked him up, she examined him with narrowed eyes. "You smell as if you've been digging in the chef's root cellar again. What do you have to say for yourself?"

Sneaky meowed, batting at the edge of her wide-brimmed hat.

"Mm-hmm. Just as I suspected. Hamish? This little beastie needs a bath." She scratched under Sneaky's white chin before letting him climb down and dash off in the opposite direction of Hamish.

"Yes, Missus." There was no amusement in his twitching eyes as he went to chase after the cat.

"Now you," Aunt Julia said, turning back to Florence. "You've had quite a morning. You've been out all night and somehow you are still on your feet. I demand you get some rest at once and I don't want to see you downstairs until dinnertime. I think saving one's life ought to earn you at least a little shut-eye. I myself will be getting some much-needed rest. In a proper bed."

"You make it sound much more glamorous than it really was, Auntie. Only a dunce goes and pulls a stunt like I did, only to get herself knocked out," Florence explained. She couldn't have the others thinking she did something outrageous and brave. All she really felt like was someone who had simply directed the police to the right door.

"Your intent, as far as I know it, was to clear my name. That alone makes you plenty brave in my book." Aunt Julia's lips pulled thin. "And that is enough talking. More sleeping. Ginny, please see to it that the draperies in my room are all pulled closed. I don't want to be blinded when I try to go to sleep."

The two of them made their way upstairs, with Aunt Julia throwing one last look back at Florence, urging her to move along too.

"I've got some things to go pick up from the market as it is," Benny finally said, fixing his hat. "I'm glad you're feeling better, though."

Florence smiled in spite of herself. "It's strangely better certainly, but it beats the searing headache from last night, was it? I've honestly lost all track of time at this point. I can hardly tell up from down."

"Definitely count some sheep then." Benny went to turn toward the carriage house but Florence reached out to put her hand on his shoulder.

"Wait. Two things, if you'll allow me before I go."

That seemed to catch his attention plenty, and he faced her, his dark brows knitted curiously. "All right."

"First thing's first. What happened to Lucky Marty? Do you know? I was just wondering if he ended up with someone else, if someone was going to be able to take care of him, or..." She swallowed hard. "I just wanted to make sure he would be okay. I can't imagine what happens with dogs in a situation like this."

Benny's dark eyes seemed to sparkle as he nodded along. "Oh yeah, that's been sorted. With them busting the place, everyone skedaddled with their dogs for the most part, trying not to catch fines or jail time even. But your favorite mutt was left behind. Wait, wait," he said, holding up his hands as Florence bit her lip with worry. "Emiliano made a call and our cousin Nate—"

"Another cousin?" she said with a laugh.

He simply shrugged, smiling at her in that good-natured way of his. "What can I say? I got a big family. Anyway, Nate's the one with all the land in Ellicottville. He's driving down this weekend to come get that poor guy and take him back home with him. Lucky Marty's finally getting his lucky break."

"Oh, that's wonderful news! Phew, I'm so glad to hear it. He seemed so sweet, and any poor creature being cared for by a murderer deserves better than that," she said, grateful for the weight of worry being lifted from her shoulders.

Benny nodded. "Absolutely. Now, you said there were two things?"

She had, hadn't she? It was funny because what she'd meant to say escaped her for a moment as he looked at her expectantly. His dark eyelashes touched his cheekbones, she realized. They were rather lovely, actually.

"I wanted to say thank you," she finally said, a moment too late for him not to notice her staring. "For helping me and for getting me out of there when I'd really gone and put my foot right in it."

Benny shrugged, but there was no mistaking the deep red tinge in his face. "Ah, it was nothing. It's what any friend would do, I think."

"Still," she said softly, not wanting him to downplay it. "I appreciate it. Who knows what would have happened if you hadn't found me when you did?"

"You don't need to thank me, Florence. But, it was my pleasure to help you. Whenever you need it, it's always there," Benny said, sticking out his hand.

She shook it and grinned. "I'll hold you to that."

He was already headed out of the grand room when he flashed another smile. "I hope you do."

❦

SHE KNEW she was meant to be sleeping and, in fact, she'd tried to lie down and shut her eyes, but she was wide awake for the time being. She thought of picking up the library's copy of *The Secret of Chimneys*, but decided that she wasn't fully coherent enough for any reading. Though...

Florence pulled up a seat at her writing desk and stared down at the page, thinking for a moment. The sheepish feeling that had slowly dawned on her earlier about not having written Bernice just yet was turning into an anxious excitement of trying to find the right words to say.

She grabbed the fountain pen and dipped it in the inkwell and carefully began the most scandalous letter she'd ever written in her life.

MY DEAREST BERNICE,

I'D SAY I'm sorry for having taken so long to write you, but I'm not. And you won't be cross with me over it either when I tell you what I'm about to tell you...

❦

THANK you for reading THE CURIOUS CASE OF FLORENCE WINTERS! Florence's story continues in **A FORTUNE MOST DEADLY**... Florence never believed in fate or destiny, but after a mysterious fortune reading turns deadly, she might just be a believer and a suspect. **Join May's newsletter** and receive the prequel short story, **A Letter Most Curious**, to find out what more about Florence's life in Ohio.

IF YOU LIKE THIS BOOK...

Like This Book?

Tap here to leave a review now!

ABOUT THE AUTHOR

May Bridges is the author of the Florence Winters Mystery series, set in NYC in the 1920s
- where high society can be deadly!
She also has a deep love of history and reading. Put them together with a twist of a mystery and you have her books!
You can find her with her nose in a book, with a paint brush in her hand, or with a messy bun on her head.

Click the "+ Follow" button underneath the logo to follow May on Amazon here:
Amazon

You can also find her on BookBub here:
BookBub

Find her on TikTok here:
TikTok

And Facebook, Instagram, and Goodreads here:

Printed in Great Britain
by Amazon